The helicopter h[...] then crashed into the roof

As Selin stood staring at the chopper, his mouth agape, the Executioner brought the Desert Eagle into target acquisition.

The helicopter burst suddenly into flames and a wall of fire swept across the roof, forcing Bolan down. Selin dived onto his belly, the remote-control detonator falling from his hand and skittering to a halt a few feet away.

The flames from the explosion passed over the warrior's head and burned out. He vaulted back to his feet and swung the big .44 toward Selin as the man scrambled on his hands and knees toward the detonator, his eyes gleaming with madness as he finally grasped the control in both hands. The Executioner saw the tendons flex in the terrorist's wrist and squeezed the trigger.

The eruption from the chapel below started as a low rumble. The building trembled, throwing the warrior's shot high and to the right. Bolan felt his legs give way as a wide fissure opened beneath him.

As smoke rose and flying debris slammed into his body, Bolan plummeted into the exploding castle, face-to-face with Sigrid Selin.

MACK BOLAN®

The Executioner

#140 Wild Card	Stony Man Doctrine
#141 Direct Hit	Terminal Velocity
#142 Fatal Error	Resurrection Day
#143 Helldust Cruise	Dirty War
#144 Whipsaw	Flight 741
#145 Chicago Payoff	Dead Easy
#146 Deadly Tactics	Sudden Death
#147 Payback Game	Rogue Force
#148 Deep and Swift	Tropic Heat
#149 Blood Rules	Fire in the Sky
#150 Death Load	Anvil of Hell
#151 Message to Medellín	Flash Point
#152 Combat Stretch	Flesh and Blood
#153 Firebase Florida	Moving Target
#154 Night Hit	Tightrope
#155 Hawaiian Heat	Blowout
#156 Phantom Force	Blood Fever
#157 Cayman Strike	Knockdown
#158 Firing Line	Assault
#159 Steel and Flame	Backlash
#160 Storm Warning	Siege
#161 Eye of the Storm	Blockade
#162 Colors of Hell	Evil Kingdom
#163 Warrior's Edge	Counterblow
#164 Death Trail	Hardline
#165 Fire Sweep	Firepower
#166 Assassin's Creed	Storm Burst
#167 Double Action	Intercept
#168 Blood Price	Lethal Impact
#169 White Heat	Deadfall
#170 Baja Blitz	Onslaught
#171 Deadly Force	
#172 Fast Strike	
#173 Capitol Hit	
#174 Battle Plan	
#175 Battle Ground	

DON PENDLETON'S
THE EXECUTIONER®
FEATURING
MACK BOLAN®

BATTLE GROUND

A GOLD EAGLE BOOK FROM
W★RLDWIDE®

TORONTO • NEW YORK • LONDON
AMSTERDAM • PARIS • SYDNEY • HAMBURG
STOCKHOLM • ATHENS • TOKYO • MILAN
MADRID • WARSAW • BUDAPEST • AUCKLAND

First edition July 1993

ISBN 0-373-61175-7

Special thanks and acknowledgment to
Jerry VanCook for his contribution to this work.

BATTLE GROUND

Freedom all solace to man gives;
He lives at ease that freely lives.
—John Barbour,
The Bruce, c. 1375

...I call upon all who love freedom to stand with us
now. Together we shall achieve victory.
—Dwight D. Eisenhower,
Broadcast on D-Day, June 6, 1944

Nothing worthwhile ever comes easy, and the price
of freedom is often high. The battles take their toll
and are hard won. But it's worth it.
—Mack Bolan

To those who dedicate their lives
to the cause of Freedom

1

The ancient stone walls of Castle Larsborg's chapel held a coldness. The mourners who had come to pay their last respects to South Haakovian President Edvaard Varkaus, the armed castle security guards and the U.S. Special Forces soldiers who circled the walls appeared to be just as cold. The closed casket stood at the front of the room below the pulpit. Six-foot candle holders flanked Varkaus's remains, but neither of the candles had been lighted.

The television cameras at the rear of the room all pointed toward the coffin. The faces in the congregation stared woodenly in the same direction, as the minds behind those faces contemplated the future of their homeland. The voices of the few who dared whisper held the frightened edge of people who knew that the cease-fire in the civil war between North and South Haakovia was only temporary. The fighting might resume any moment.

A tall well-built figure in a navy suit and burgundy tie stood at the rear of the chapel, his back pressed against the chilly stone. He held his hands loosely at his sides, his face expressionless. To the casual observer he appeared to be one of the funeral directors. But even the semitrained eye would have picked up discrepancies—the man's face was too hard, his eyes too penetrating, too experienced, to be those of a mortician. This man had seen the world, its good, as well as its evil. He had seen more death than an army of funeral directors, but his visions of death had been from a different point of view.

An expert in law enforcement or espionage would have noticed other inconsistencies. The professional would have known that the unbuttoned jacket was to enable the man easy access to his weapons. But it was unlikely that even the most seasoned investigator would have noticed more. Certainly no one would have known that the man going by the name of Colonel Rance Pollock was actually Mack Bolan, a.k.a. the Executioner.

The weapons responsible for the unbuttoned jacket were Bolan's trademark Beretta 93-R and Desert Eagle .44 Magnum. The Beretta, holding fifteen rounds of semijacketed hollowpoint 9 mm parabellums, rested under his arm in a weathered leather shoulder rig. The Desert Eagle rode in a sleek "pancake" holster, close against his right hip. Except when the situation prevented it, Bolan wore both guns with no more thought than most man give to putting on a tie. They had become a part of him over the years, extensions of the real weapons on which he relied: his training, instincts and mind.

The Executioner's eyes scanned the chapel methodically, noting the familiar faces of many of the men and women in the pews. Some represented foreign democracies. Other faces belonged to top officials of the South Haakovian government. Near the front, across from Edvaard Varkaus's immediate family, sat the pallbearers. Two were Haakovian, childhood friends of the late president. Two more had come from Finland to the north, and the last pair were compatriots from neighboring Baltic republics.

Turning his eyes to the door, Bolan watched as a man wearing the uniform of a Latvian navy admiral stepped through the metal detector. The detectors had been set up knowing that Franzen Stensvik, the dictator of North Haakovia and catalyst behind Varkaus's assassination by Dag Vaino, might bring mayhem to the funeral, as well.

Bolan frowned as more people passed through the security check and were ushered to seats. Janyte Varkaus, who had replaced her husband as leader of the country, had stubbornly vetoed the body search the Executioner had suggested, feeling it might embarrass or insult the visiting dignitaries. Even the use of the metal detectors had taken a good deal of persuasion from the Executioner.

A trio of elderly women passed through the instrument. Bolan knew metal detectors well. They were good, but not perfect. Knives, bludgeons—even firearms—could be constructed from materials their sensors didn't pick up.

The sharp bark of a dog suddenly broke the uneasy silence within the chapel. The Executioner glanced past the metal detectors to the hall and saw a uniformed South Haakovian K-9 handler and his German shepherd. The pair stopped just outside the door.

Bolan looked back to the front of the chapel as an aging man with blue-gray hair slid behind the organ and struck the first few chords of a funeral dirge. The Executioner turned to the Latvian admiral who sat at

the front. The funeral director who had seated him, a
frail, half-bald man in a black suit, exited into the hall.

As he passed the German shepherd, the dog suddenly snarled. Then, with a vicious growl, the animal
leaped onto the man, knocking him past the doorway
and out of the Executioner's view.

A high-pitched bloodcurdling scream echoed from
the hall, and all heads within the chapel swiveled toward the commotion.

Bolan had already reached the opening. He dashed
into the corridor to see the tiny funeral director pinned
to the floor on his back. The German shepherd's jaws
encircled the man's throat as the K-9 officer strained
on the end of the leash, calling out an order in Haakovian and trying to pull the dog off the struggling
man.

The German shepherd obeyed. The funeral director rose unsteadily to his knees, his thin hair in disar-
ray and flopping over his forehead.

"I am sorry," the dog handler said. "Bjorn is usually—"

The German shepherd cut him off with another
snarl, then lunged forward to clasp the funeral man's
hand between his jaws.

The little man screamed again, then sobbed as Bolan and the dog's master pried the teeth away from his
flesh.

The K-9 officer turned to the Executioner. "I do not
understand it," he said, embarrassed. "Bjorn is not
trained to attack. He is a bomb dog."

Bolan's head snapped toward the trainer. "What?"

"I said—"

The Executioner didn't wait for an answer. His hand shot out and grasped the funeral director's collar.

"What...are you doing?" the frightened man stuttered.

"What's your name?" Bolan growled.

"What?"

"Your name!"

Bubbles of saliva appeared at the corners of the man's mouth. When he spoke, it sounded as if he were choking. "Jansen."

Several American Special Forces soldiers hurried to the Executioner's side, and the warrior recognized a sergeant named Orwig. "Frisk this man and keep him here," he ordered, passing the funeral director into the Green Beret's grip. He turned to the dog handler. "Take Bjorn inside and see what he finds."

"But we searched the chapel earlier today. There was nothing—"

Bjorn interrupted him with another sudden bark. The dog jerked forward, pulling his master along on the end of the leash.

The organist quit playing. Murmurs of disapproval over the breach in propriety rose from the congregation.

The dog pulled his master across the chapel floor directly to the casket. Bolan and several of the Green Berets men followed. The dog raised his front paws and rested them on the closed lid. His snout traveled along the crack, sniffing.

Bolan stepped up to the coffin and pushed the dog's trainer to the side. "Keep Bjorn back."

The officer issued another order, and the dog dropped to the ground and sat back on his haunches.

Carefully the Executioner flipped the latch and began to raise the lid.

The grumbles from the congregation became gasps.

Bolan was suddenly aware of another presence at his side. "What are you doing?" Janyte Varkaus demanded, her voice a mixture of shock and anger.

The Executioner turned. The new South Haakovian president's pale blue eyes stared intently up at him. "Trying to save your life," he replied, then turned back to the coffin. He raised the lid higher and felt a soft tug. Squatting, he peered into the opening and saw a thin metal wire attached to the underside of the lid. The wire's other end was out of sight beneath the side of the casket.

Bolan dropped the lid carefully back in place and turned to the Green Berets behind him. "Clear the chapel," he ordered. "Get these people downstairs to the first floor. But seal the exits. Nobody, and I don't care who it is, leaves." He turned back to Janyte Varkaus, then nodded toward the soldiers. "Go with them."

"But—"

"No 'buts,' Madam President," Bolan said. "There's a bomb inside the casket. And it was put here for *you.*"

As the American soldiers began clearing the room, Bolan dropped to his knees next to the casket. Slowly he lifted the lid again and the wire became visible. His hand moved cautiously into the coffin.

A small round device held the end of the wire to the lid of the coffin—a detonator. Bolan's fingers traced carefully down the wire and came to rest on Edvaard Varkaus's chest. The other end of the wire was attached to the second button of the late president's coat.

Returning to the coffin lid, the Executioner took a deep breath, then pulled the wire. It snapped off into his hand. Behind him, he heard excited voices as South Haakovian castle guards joined the Green Berets in evacuating the room. Ignoring the noise, he focused on the coffin, squinting into the darkened box. No more wires.

Bolan raised the lid, fixed it in place and studied the body. Varkaus's eyes were closed. The skull had been reconstructed, but a tiny gray dent on the right temple marked the spot where Dag Vaino's bullet had struck. Carefully the Executioner ran his hands under the body searching for dynamite, plastique, nitro— whatever explosive Bjorn's trained senses had picked up.

He found nothing.

The Executioner's hand traveled lightly across Varkaus's chest to the wire in the jacket button. Slowly he unbuttoned the coat, then the shirt beneath it.

The wire disappeared into the abdominal wall of the late president's body.

Bolan's eyebrows dropped in concentration as he studied the coat button. It didn't match the two above it, or those on the cuffs. His fingers traced gently over the rounded surface. Metal.

Another detonator.

Bolan straightened and stepped back.

The explosives, whatever they were, were inside Edvaard Varkaus. And without opening up the chest cavity, the Executioner had no idea how to disarm the device.

The problem was compounded by the fact that he'd found two detonators so far. That meant there could be a hundred more hidden on, or in, the body, ready to be set off by any number of means.

There was no time to look.

What sounded like thunder suddenly rocked the walls of the chapel. Two of the windows shattered, bringing a chorus of screams from the mourners still filing out of the room. Then more dull thuds pounded in the distance as Bolan hurried to the nearest window.

Staring through the splintered glass, he saw flames leaping high into the air ten miles to the north.

The staccato sounds of distant small-arms fire joined the explosions. The mourners in the chapel froze silently in their tracks. Then the screams returned as the worst fears of the people of South Haakovia were finally realized.

The war had begun again.

AUTOMATIC RIFLEFIRE sailed over, under and around David McCarter, and a thousand scrambled thoughts flew through his mind as he dived off the retaining wall above Helsinki's South Harbor.

The thoughts began with memories of his childhood in London. Then quick flashes of his time at Sandhurst Military Academy entered his head before giving way to recollections from his tour of duty in the British army. His transfer to the Special Air Service came next, jumbled between remembrances of the prototype road-racing vehicles he had test-driven, the hundreds of airplanes he had flown and the faces of several women.

Last, McCarter thought of the final phase of his life, the most important and enriching of all—the years he had spent battling terrorism with Phoenix Force. As his head hit the dark black water of the harbor, he wondered who the masters of Stony Man Farm would choose to replace him.

Because David McCarter had no doubt he was about to die.

The sudden shock of the frigid water threatened to stop his heart as the Briton plummeted beneath the surface. The gunfire from the dock continued. Bullets sizzled through the water beside him, their bubbly wakes looking like tails. He sank, the weight of the weapons and the soaked coat dragging him toward the bottom. For a moment his mind threatened to freeze with his limbs.

He tried to swim, forcing first his arms, then his near-paralyzed legs to forge ahead through the black wall of water. Still he sank, and as his mind cleared further, he stripped off the dirty gray overcoat filled with loose 9 mm ammo. The Sterling submachine gun, slung over his right shoulder, went next. Still McCarter sank, and he finally dropped the twin Browning Hi-Powers, then slid the "six-pack" of extra magazines from his belt and let them fall.

Lungs bursting, he began to rise slowly. He leveled off and began to swim, angling away from the dock.

At least he thought it was away from the dock. The impact against the water and sudden temperature drop had disoriented him, and he wondered if he might not be swimming back toward the gunfire and certain death. But he had no choice. Wherever he was, he was still within range of the Finnish police's autorifles.

The Finns had mistaken him and the rest of Phoenix Force for members of Dag Vaino's Helsinki terrorist cell, and if he didn't get outside the range of their guns, it would make little difference whether he was shot at a hundred yards or ten.

Finally McCarter's lungs vowed to breathe—regardless of whether they took in oxygen or water. He struggled up, the sunlight brightening the water's hue with each labored stroke. The black became a light shade of gray, then his head burst past the surface into the sun.

Gunfire erupted from shore as McCarter gasped for breath. He twisted a quick 360 degrees to get his bearings as the rounds drilled into the water around him. Snatching a lung full of oxygen, he flipped into a surface dive and headed back down into the freezing depths of the harbor.

McCarter forced his brain back in gear as he stroked blindly on. Where was he going? What was the nearest of the islands within the harbor? Valkasaari? No, Valkasaarenkari. If he could just make it there...

The former SAS commando concentrated on Valkasaarenkari, letting it take his mind off his frozen bones and the burning in his chest, refusing to fall prey to the certainty that he'd never make it, that the island was simply too far away.

No! Bloody hell no! He had been in tight situations before. It came with the territory when you worked for Stony Man. He had made it before, he would make it again.

McCarter's lungs screamed again, and his body moved toward the surface of its own accord. He gagged as his head broke through, spitting as he gasped for oxygen amid new volleys of rifle and subgun fire.

A round streaked past his ear, and McCarter felt its heat. The odor of singed hair filled his nostrils as he dived to safety once more.

The Briton swam on, knowing he was slowing down, that his limbs were moving ever more sluggishly as the icy water took its toll. His frozen, exhausted muscles moved now by willpower alone, and again the certainty of death filled his brain.

Somewhere in the distance, McCarter heard the chugging of a small boat. The harbor patrol. The police had notified them, and they were headed his way.

Would they kill him outright or attempt to capture him alive? McCarter didn't know. But he knew capture meant interrogation.

He swam on, thankful that it would be Finnish police officers he would be dealing with and not Vaino's terrorists. Finland was a civilized country. They would interrogate. Vaino and his men would have tortured.

McCarter's arms and legs suddenly stopped moving as a horrifying possibility forced its way into his thoughts. Yes, Finland was civilized—at least during peace time. But with Dag Vaino's terrorists shooting up the streets, the assassination of Finnish parliament member Risto Kalle, and the threat that North Haakovia might invade at any time, these were hardly peaceful times.

These were times that might make police officers change their interrogative procedures, times when some officers might easily rationalize torture.

McCarter stroked to the surface, gasped for air and dived again. Would they resort to torture? Would *he* if the security of his country depended on it? Perhaps. He didn't know. There was no way to be sure—about himself or the Finns.

And he couldn't take the chance. Every man had his breaking point, and if they found his he might give up information that would result in the deaths of his teammates.

David McCarter made his decision in a heartbeat. He couldn't let that happen. He dived into the depths of the harbor, the inky blackness covering him like a blanket. He felt the pressure on his ears and sinuses, then a giddy euphoria replaced his reasoning. McCarter felt himself smiling underwater as his thoughts turned to a Jack London novel he had read as a boy. *Martin Edan.* The protagonist had ended his life exactly the way he was about to.

When his arms and legs finally gave out, McCarter floated weightlessly for a moment in the water. The fire still filled his lungs, but now it seemed almost pleasant. He couldn't remember for sure, but it seemed like Martin Edan had experienced the same feeling. Edan had killed himself to escape boredom and depression. At least McCarter's reason for ending his own life was more honorable.

The Briton allowed himself one final thought, wondering about the afterlife. Then he opened his mouth and sucked at the water as if it were the regulator on a scuba tank.

ROOM 307, on the top floor of Helsinki's downtown Grand Hotel, was an eclectic mixture of Scandinavia and America. At first glance the room would have looked right at home in the Holiday Inn in Billings,

Montana or Davenport, Iowa. A subtle floral bedspread covered the honey-colored wooden bed, a matching desk rested against the opposing wall and a television set had been bolted to the top of the short, light brown chest of drawers to its side. A sliding glass door at the rear of the room led to a small balcony that overlooked the swimming pool and tennis court.

But small things throughout the hotel room betrayed its location. The Finnish crystal drinking glasses and water pitcher, while being inexpensive "seconds" from a factory in nearby Vaasa, would have cost a fortune had they been transported all the way to the United States. Intricate wood carvings from Lapland hung from the walls instead of the usual discounthouse prints found in American hotels, and hand woven Finnish folk rugs had taken the place of massproduced carpeting.

The men seated around room 307 weren't ignorant, nor were they completely devoid of culture and refinement. They had astutely noticed the differences, but passed them off. They had other things on their minds.

Such as the status of their teammate, David McCarter.

Yakov Katzenelenbogen, or "Katz" as he was known to the rest of the men of Phoenix Force, stood in front of the television at the front of the room. "So the last you saw of him, he was headed toward the harbor?" he asked Rafael Encizo, who was seated on the edge of the bed.

"In the marketplace under heavy fire. He had nowhere else to go."

Katz nodded as he looked toward the sliding door. Calvin James sat in front of the glass at a circular table. Gary Manning, the other member of Phoenix Force, had left an hour earlier to retrieve the rented station wagon he had hidden before the assassination and ensuing gunfight at Helsinki's city hall. "Calvin, you see anything?"

"Saw him head that way. Then I made myself scarce, too."

A soft tapping sounded on the door to the hall, and Katz drew his Beretta 92-S from under his shirt. He moved noiselessly across the rug to the peephole, looked through, then opened the door.

Manning walked in. The big Canadian carried two rucksacks slung over his shoulders.

"You got the wagon and the clothes?" Katz asked.

Manning nodded, dropped the rucksacks on the bed and took the chair next to James.

"Any problems?"

"Uh-uh. Looks like things have died down."

Katz eyed his team. They wore clothing depicting the emblems of American professional and college football teams—the current rage in Scandinavia—and overcoats taken off the bodies of some of Dag Vaino's men who had fallen to the guns of Phoenix Force. Their faces were strained, tired.

They should be tired, Katz thought. During the past twenty-four hours, they had infiltrated Finland, confronted border guards, made their way inland to Helsinki, attacked two cells of terrorists, and then been chased through the streets of the city by police who had mistaken them for terrorists themselves.

But the weariness in the eyes of Encizo, Manning and James wasn't what worried Katzenelenbogen at the moment.

It was the guilt he saw in those same eyes.

Katz understood that guilt—he carried his own. All of the members of Phoenix Force wished there had been something, *anything,* they could have done to help David McCarter.

The problem was, there hadn't been.

The leader of Phoenix Force knew it was time to put a stop to it. If they were to have any chance at all of finding the Briton now, they would have to clear both their consciences and minds.

"I should have followed him when I saw him heading toward the water," James said suddenly, putting all of their feelings into words. "I could have—"

"That's enough!" Katz snapped. "This is nobody's fault. We all play the cards we're dealt, and David would be the first to tell you so." He paused, staring down into James's worried brown eyes. "And the SAS gets its share of water training, Calvin. At least enough so that they don't need an ex-SEAL towing them to shore."

James nodded.

Katz raised his wrist and looked at his watch. "It's as safe out there as it's going to get. I don't know if David's alive or dead, but I think it's about time we found out." He glanced toward the rucksacks on the bed. "The police may remember the sweatshirts. Change into something they haven't seen, and get your weapons ready."

Their weapons were always ready. Encizo, James and Manning all carried a Beretta 92-S, matching backups and extra mags. Katz watched them double-check the handguns as he did the same with his tiny Steyr machine pistol and own handgun.

James broke open one of the rucksacks. He traded his Chicago Bear sweatshirt for a rumpled black turtleneck as Manning doffed his red University of Oklahoma jacket and pulled a navy T-shirt over his beefy shoulders. Encizo settled for a beige three-button pullover rugby shirt, dropping onto the bed the Los Angeles Raiders starter jacket he'd worn. The men kept their faded Levi's, and once more used the terrorists overcoats to cover their side arms and subguns.

Katz stayed in the striped coveralls he'd worn to pose as a repairman. He nodded as soon as the men were ready, and the other three warriors of Phoenix Force rose and followed their leader out the door and down the stairs to the street.

Before the confrontation outside city hall, Katz had insisted that Manning ditch the station wagon far from the scene. He had known they would need transport later, and there was no sense getting the vehicle "burned" to the police. Manning had earlier parked it in the lot next to the swimming pool, and the men from Stony Man Farm climbed inside, the big Canadian behind the wheel.

Twenty minutes later, Manning turned onto Norra Esplanaden.

"Cruise by city hall, then turn back toward the harbor," Katz ordered. "I want to get a feel for whether it's still being watched."

Manning drove on, passing the presidential palace. Ahead, Katz saw city hall, where Risto Kalle had been assassinated earlier in the day. Beyond that stood the tourist information office, and the Israeli's eyes went automatically to the window two floors down from the roof, from which Dag Vaino had fired the fatal shot.

The Canadian took a right at the corner, circled the block and pulled to a halt in the market area in front of the harbor. Most of the booths and stalls selling flowers, fruits and local crafts were in the process of closing for the night, with the merchants loading their wares into boxes and crates.

An uneasy feeling entered the pit of Katz's stomach. "Anybody see any sign of police?"

Three heads shook a negative.

Katz watched a tall blond Finn scoop whortleberries from his cart into a refrigerated box. Just because the cops couldn't be seen didn't mean they weren't there.

"Okay," the former Mossad agent said. "Get out and make your way toward the harbor. See if you can pick up anything that might tell us what happened to David."

Phoenix Force exited the station wagon, the musky odor of the harbor water filling their nostrils. They split up, automatically fanning out without having to be told, their eyes searching the ground, the carts, the stalls, for anything that might lead them to McCarter.

Katz moved through the market area as the merchants continued to close for the night. One by one, they finished transferring their goods to the pickup trucks and flatbeds scattered throughout the area. Padlocks clamped shut, securing the doors and serving windows of their stalls.

The smell of the water grew stronger as Katz neared the harbor. His eyes caught a flash of red on top of the retaining wall circling the water, and he quickened his pace. The sick feeling in his gut grew into full-blown nausea as the red object became distinguishable.

A bright red University of Oklahoma sweater.

The one David McCarter had worn during the battle outside city hall.

The Israeli stopped next to the wall. Suddenly the sorrow in his breast became apprehension as he realized McCarter wouldn't have had time to remove the sweater before diving into the harbor.

Katz's hand moved cautiously under his coat toward the Steyr as he turned back away from the water. Something was wrong. The merchants were busy. *Too* busy? The fear in his heart suddenly rose to his brain, crystallizing into coherent, discernible thought. None of the merchants seemed even to have noticed him, Encizo, James or Manning. And the men of Phoenix Force were the only human beings in the marketplace who weren't closing up shop for the day.

Surely four men threading their way through the area warranted at least a casual glance of curiosity.

The rest of the men from Stony Man Farm joined Katz as he turned back to the water-soaked sweater, the understanding of the trap into which he'd just fallen suddenly coming over him like a wave. He looked up into the face of Gary Manning, who nodded back toward the merchants.

"I'd say we just screwed up," the big Canadian said.

Katz turned toward the merchants. They had spread out, cutting off all paths back to the street. Led by the tall blond man who had been storing his whortleberries for the night, a dozen or so started toward the wall.

The Israeli glanced back toward the water, the old expression "between the devil and the deep blue sea" passing through his mind. "I'd say you were right."

Pistols and subguns suddenly appeared in the hands of the merchants. The big blond stepped forward, pressing the barrel of a Lahti 9 mm into Katz's chest. He drew the lapel of his trench coat to the side with his other hand as a satisfied smile of success covered his face.

He spoke first in Finnish. Getting no response, he switched to English. "I am Lieutenant Andersson," he said in a hoarse, gravelly voice. "And you, sir, are under arrest."

2

Harmony Cove was well named.

A cool breeze floated in from the Straits of Florida, making the 85-degree temperature within the secluded estuary on Key West feel ten degrees cooler. Bananas, breadfruit, plantain and papayas swayed in the currents, and here and there trees sprouting Seville oranges, limes, coconuts, mangos and almonds grew wild.

The sleepy breeze and colorful dangling fruit gave the cove an Edenlike atmosphere that seemed to promise peace, plenty and placidity to all who looked upon its splendor.

The warriors of Able Team knew better.

Hidden within the trees between Hermann "Gadgets" Schwarz, Rosario "Politician" Blancanales and Leo Turrin, former LAPD detective Carl Lyons pressed the binoculars to his eyes. The fingers of his other hand tapped the walkie-talkie on his belt. "Able One to Birdman," he whispered into the wraparound mike in front of his face. "You there, Charlie?"

From the landing strip several miles away, Stony Man Farm pilot Charlie Mott's voice came back. "Affirmative, Ironman. Ready and willing."

"Keep your motor running. We don't know exactly how this gig will go down. I want our asses covered from all angles."

Static sounded in Lyon's ear as another microphone was keyed, then Aaron "The Bear" Kurtzman's voice was relayed through the satellite hookup from Stony Man Farm. "The sub's coming around the bend right now, Ironman. Beginning to surface."

"Roger." The words had barely left his lips when he saw a glimmer of metal on the sunlit water.

The Soviet Mike-class submarine broke surface.

Lyons's voice lowered. "Any word from Delta Force yet, Bear?"

"On their way," Kurtzman replied. "I got in touch as we figured out the sub's destination. They should arrive within the hour."

"Roger." Lyons let the binoculars fall to the end of the strap. The sub was close, maybe fifty yards away. He wouldn't need the field glasses anymore. The Able Team leader's hand moved slowly to the M-16A2 slung over his shoulder.

Damn good chance he'd need it, though.

Lyons watched as the sub continued to surface. He knew from Stony Man intel that several of the Mike-class vessels had been in dock at Lenin naval base in North Haakovia when the Soviet Union had dissolved. North Haakovian President Franzen Stensvik had fallen heir to them. The mad dictator had used this one to transport whatever it was he was distributing throughout Scandinavia, Western Europe and now the Americas.

Constructed of nonmagnetic titanium, the Mike had been undetectable by tracking devices such as airborne MAD and bottom-laid coils, but Kurtzman had been able to follow its every move across the Atlantic thanks to the homing device Mack Bolan had attached to one of the mysterious crates the sub carried.

What *was* in the crates? Lyons wondered again as the vessel docked in the middle of the narrow bay and the hatch opened. That was the sixty-four-thousand-dollar question. Whatever it was, it appeared to be payment for the massive quantity of cocaine Bolan had discovered in North Haakovia.

Or was it that simple? Lyons had been a cop too many years to take anything at surface value.

"Do I hear something, Ironman?"

Lyons turned toward Schwarz who was next to him. Able Team's electronic genius had cocked an ear and hooked a thumb over his shoulder, pointing back toward the road on the other side of the thick foliage.

"Yeah. Me too." The second whispering voice came from Lyons's other side. Blancanales, the third member of Able Team, knelt next to Leo Turrin, the Justice Department undercover ace who had used his extensive network of mafia contacts to establish the link between Stensvik and the Medellín cartel.

Lyons drew in a deep breath. You didn't realize just how complex the whole situation was until you lined up all the facts side by side. North Haakovian Communists, Colombian drug runners and hit teams, both North and South Haakovian statesman—they were all tied in together. Somehow.

"I hear it," Turrin said. "Sounds like a pickup. Maybe two."

The big ex-LAPD detective closed his eyes. The distant purr of approaching engines drifted into his ears. Turrin was right. More than one vehicle. Opening his eyes again, Lyons saw a trio of men climb out of the submarine onto the deck. Two of the men were light-skinned Caucasians, most likely Haakovian. The third, with darker skin, had a long, drooping, Zapata style mustache. He wore faded denim jeans tucked into black Western boots with silver toes and heel adornments.

Lyons nodded. Two Haaks and a Colombian. More evidence of a Stensvik-cartel connection. He watched the two lighter-skinned men take a crate from a pair of arms that extended it through the hatch.

The vehicles drew closer. Whatever it was Stensvik had smuggled across the Atlantic was about to be picked up. Lyons burrowed deeper into the sand around the fruit trees, keeping an eye on the road through the branches.

A gray-and-burgundy Chevy pickup suddenly appeared on the crest of a low rise. Lyons caught a glimpse of half a dozen men with assault rifles and subguns. The pickup sped past the grove and onto the beach, coming to a halt ten feet from the water. A second later, an aging brown Ford pickup flew by and parked behind the other vehicle. It, too, carried a cargo of armed men in the back.

The driver of the Chevy dropped down from the cab. The door opened on the other side, and a burly man with a florid face joined him at the water. The driver called out to the sub—too far away for Lyons to make out. One of the men on top of the Mike called back.

The rest of the gunmen jumped from the pickups and walked to the beach, their weapons slung over their shoulders in assault mode. Two of them carried an inflatable raft. A loud hiss echoed through the cove as one of the men jerked a cord and the raft inflated.

The Chevy's driver shouted again to someone on the sub as a trolling motor was attached to the raft. The stout man with the crimson complexion climbed inside.

"What do you think, Ironman?" Schwarz whispered. "Want to take them now?"

Lyons shook his head as the raft started out toward the sub. From their point of ambush, they could easily mow down the dozen or so men. But the attack would alert the men in the sub. The hatch would close, the Mike would submerge and whatever was in those crates would be gone before Able Team could even get to the water.

The Able Team leader gathered his men around him as the rubber raft bumped the side of the sub. The Colombian tied it off, then he and the two Haakovians began handing crates over the side.

"They'll load the first truck," Lyons replied. "Then my guess is it'll take off while they start loading the second. Let's work our way back out to the road. Drop down on them as they pass and find out what's in the crates. Then we'll go back and get as close to the sub as we can before they make us."

The men nodded their understanding.

The raft was soon full and puttering back to shore. The gunmen from the pickups grabbed the crates off the raft and loaded them into the back of the Chevy.

Lyons turned to Turrin. "Leo, stay here and let us know as soon as they leave." He tapped the mike in front of his face. "Tell us whether we've got one truck coming, or both."

"You got it, Ironman."

Lyons, Schwarz and Blancanales stood and made their way silently through the trees. Hitting the ground at the edge of their cover, they belly-crawled over the rise in the road before jumping back to their feet and sprinting to a tall growth of scrub grass.

The Able Team leader dropped the M-16 to the end of its sling and drew the sound-suppressed .45 Government Model from his shoulder harness. Schwarz and Blancanales both had suppressors on their Uzis, and he had no intentions of alerting the sub with the noisy assault rifle. He stretched out on the ground, the barrel of the hardballer pointed toward the road, and waited.

Five minutes later, Turrin's voice sounded in his ear. "Chevy pickup's turning around. It's alone."

Lyons breathed a silent sigh of relief. Not only would it be easier to take one truck than two, but if they'd both come together, it would have meant the sub could have left before they got back to it.

The Chevy topped the hill and started down the road. Lyons lined up the sights of the .45, aiming at a point in the road where he estimated the front tire would roll by.

A moment later, it did. The ex-cop took a deep breath, let out half of it and squeezed the trigger.

The Chevy's left front tire deflated with a loud pop, and the pickup began fishtailing through the sand.

The men of Able Team rose and sprinted toward the vehicle. Lyons squeezed the trigger again and another 230-grain hardball .45 smashed through the grille of the pickup and into the radiator. Water shot from the hole as the Chevy ground to a halt.

As soon as the tire had blown, the men in the bed of the truck had grabbed for the handrails. But as the pickup skidded to a halt, they regained their balance, looked up and raised their assault rifles.

Schwarz and Blancanales stopped in their tracks, raising the barrels of their Uzis. The Israeli subguns choked out near-silent sprays of 9 mm parabellum rounds that drilled into the chests of the gunmen.

Two of the six men fell over the sides and onto the sandy road. The other four slid down inside the truck, their weapons clanging against the metal bed.

Lyons sprinted toward the window in the cab and stuck the .45 through the opening. He pressed the half-inch hole in the end of the barrel against the driver's temple. Casting a cold stare across the truck to the man riding shotgun, he barked "Freeze."

The men obliged.

"Now raise your hands. Slow."

The burly driver's eyes strained to the corners of the sockets, trying to get a look at the gun against his head. Lyons kept one eye on him, the other on the passenger. "Gadgets, check the back. Find out what we've got in the crates." In his peripheral vision he saw Schwarz vault the side of the pickup.

The sound of a low-flying plane pricked the Able Team leader's ears as he waited. The distinctive twin engines roared louder as it neared. He turned away from the cab long enough to glance toward Harmony Cove.

Above the water, he saw a Grumman Mallard descending.

Still in the bed of the truck, Schwarz moved toward the cab. He opened his mouth, but before he could speak, the second pickup suddenly appeared on top of the hill.

"Get down!" Lyons yelled. As soon as the words were out of his mouth, the driver clawed for hardware. The big ex-cop fired two silenced rounds, taking out both men before dropping to a squatting position behind the truck. Blancanales joined him as he jerked the partially empty magazine from his weapon and reloaded.

Schwarz took a sitting position in the truck, fading in with the dead men who sat along the rails. He faced away from the road, his Uzi held barrel upward. "Careful!" he whispered. "Make damn sure you don't hit the crates!"

Lyons wondered briefly what that meant, then his thoughts turned to Leo Turrin. Why hadn't he radioed, warned them that the second truck was coming?

As the Ford neared, the former cop glanced down to the walkie-talkie on his belt. It gave him his answer. The wire leading to the headset bobbed freely over his thigh.

Somewhere during the commotion, it had come unplugged.

On the other side of the Chevy, Lyons heard the Ford slow. The driver had spotted the stalled pickup, and the men sitting in the back. Now, if he'd just get close enough before he realized what had happened. . . .

Lyons jabbed the plug back into the radio as he waited. Turrin's frantic voice came over the airwaves.

"Able Team! Ironman...dammit, come in Able Team!"

He had no time to respond.

The Ford ground to halt on the other side of the Chevy, and Lyons heard someone say, "What's wrong?"

Before they could say more, he and Blancanales rose to their feet. Lyons steadied the Government Model on the window well and tapped the trigger, firing through the opposite opening. Two .45s tore through the face of the Ford's driver. A third took out the man sitting next to him.

He saw Blancanales and Schwarz sending steady streams of quiet 9 mm rounds into the back of the second truck.

Lyons jerked the .45 out of the cab and rested it on the rail. Carefully avoiding Schwarz, he sent three 230-grain hardballs through the leather jacket of one of the men in the back of the Ford. Another trio blasted the chest of a gunner in a plaid shirt, sending the man flipping backward out of truck.

"The crates, dammit!" Schwarz warned again. "Don't hit the crates!"

Lyons squeezed the trigger twice more, emptying his pistol. As the slide locked open, he jammed another fresh load up the grips and thumbed the slide release. He wondered again what Gadgets had found.

The Able Team leader aimed at center mass in the rear of the Ford, cutting loose with another half-mag of .45 autos. Gadgets and Pol continued firing, and a near-visible wall of .45s and 9 mm rounds saturated the last man who still stood in the back of the Ford.

Suddenly Harmony Cove was again silent.

Then Turrin's hushed voice whispered frantically into Lyons's ear once more. "Come in, dammit! Ironman, a seaplane has landed. They're loading more crates onto it!"

Lyons bolted forward, sprinting down the road toward the trees that separated them from the water. He heard the thump of combat boots at his side, and glanced over to see Schwarz keeping pace. The electronics man's face was pale.

"What's in the crates?" the Able Team leader asked between breaths as they neared the trees. "Explosives?"

Schwarz let out a snort. "I wish. Each crate holds a metal canister, Carl. Some are marked Sarin. The others are soman."

Lyons felt the nausea pass through him in one sudden wave.

The ship Bolan had marked in the Baltics had made several stops in Scandinavia and northern Europe, then linked up with the submarine. The sub itself had been to Portugal before coming to Key West.

Both vessels had undoubtedly connected to smaller transports like the seaplane and pickups at each stop.

Sarin and soman. Nerve agents.

Franzen Stensvik was distributing chemical death throughout the world.

BOLAN TURNED AWAY from the chapel window as yet another bomb fell in the distance. He sprinted across the room to the door where Green Beret Corporal Ted Lelchuk was pushing the last of the mourners through the door. The Executioner shoved past Lelchuk to where Sergeant Orwig stood guarding the funeral director. He grabbed the little man by the lapels of his coat, lifted him into the air and slammed his back against the stone wall of the castle hall.

"Jansen, I don't have time for decorum," Bolan said, pushing his nose against the man's. "I want to know *exactly* what went on and what part you played in it. And I want to know now."

The funeral director tried to speak, but only managed to sputter incoherently.

Bolan shook him. "Talk! You planted explosives in the body?"

Jansen nodded, his bottom lip quivering.

"What kind? What's the bomb made out of?"

The funeral director's gaze fell to the ground. "I don't know," he said, still trembling. "I know nothing of bombs. I was paid to assist . . . to open the chest wall and sew it back after—"

"Who did you assist?" Bolan demanded.

"I knew him only by the name Eremar."

"What did the bomb look like?"

"There were several," he replied almost inaudibly.

"Speak up!"

"They were small metal containers. Flat. Rectangular."

Bolan felt the muscles in his arms and shoulders tense as he continued to hold Jansen against the wall. Small, flat, rectangular metal containers that had come from North Haakovia, no doubt.

Russian-made SZ-3 demolition charges.

"How many?" Bolan asked.

"I . . . I don't know. We filled both the chest and abdominal cavities."

Enough to take out the entire chapel. And a lot more.

Bolan turned to look down the hall. Ushered by Green Berets and Haakovian castle guardsmen, most of the mourners had now descended the staircase and were on their way to the first floor. They should be safe there. The explosion would be directed up, rather than down. And beneath Castle Larsborg was a bomb shelter, not to mention an escape tunnel built centuries earlier. The tunnel led from the castle to an emergency underground command post roughly a mile away.

Bolan turned back to the funeral director. "How's the bomb going to be detonated?"

"How is . . . what?"

Bolan shook him again. "How is the bomb supposed to be set off?"

"Eremar has a box. It looks like a television remote control."

The warrior dropped the man to the floor but continued to hold him against the wall. "So you were on your way to tell Eremar that everyone was in place. Then the two of you would leave the castle and he'd set off the bomb?"

Jansen nodded.

The Executioner fought the impulse to drive a fist through the funeral director's face. The man had sold out his country, and if the bomb dog hadn't chanced by and caught a whiff of the hands that had helped place the charges inside the body, he'd have been responsible for the death of Janyte Varkaus and a hundred representatives of democracy the world over.

Bolan leaned forward, pressing the funeral director harder against the stone wall. "Where is he?" he demanded. "Where is Eremar?"

"I do not know. I was to walk down the south stairs to the front door. He would meet me somewhere along the way."

"What does he look like?"

"He was . . . tall. Almost as tall as you. He wore a mustache, but I do not think it was real."

A picture from the Stony Man Farm intel files appeared in Bolan's mind. "Any facial scars?" he asked.

"A small one," the funeral director replied. "On the left cheek. He had tried to cover it with makeup."

Bolan thought of Dag Vaino. He was tall, and known to disguise himself in beards and mustaches. But as far as he knew, the Finnish terrorist had no facial scars.

The Executioner turned back to the hall. It was clear now, except for himself, Sergeant Orwig and another sergeant named Skinner. "Orwig," the Executioner said, "take this man into custody." He grabbed the funeral director's lapel again and slung him away from the wall and into Green Beret's arms.

Turning to the other soldier, he said, "Skinner, get downstairs. Make sure the exits are sealed, and be careful. Vaino has a man somewhere in the castle."

The Green Beret nodded and took off toward the staircase.

The dull thuds of the aerial bombs grew closer as Bolan hurried down the hall toward the temporary security room that had been set up next to the chapel. Reaching inside his jacket, he jerked the walkie-talkie from his belt as he ran. "Pollock to castle guard," he said.

A moment later, a scratchy Haakovian-accented voice said, "Go ahead, Colonel."

The Executioner fished in his pocket for the card-key to the door as he answered. "Set up a search of the entire castle," he said. He pushed through the door and sat in front of the nearest computer terminal. "Either Vaino or one of his men is here, somewhere." He touched several buttons and the screen lighted up. A moment later, he had entered the code and gained access to the Stony Man files.

Eremar, no first name available, no middle name or initial, he typed, and hit Enter.

"What does he look like?" the castle security officer asked.

A two-page list of names appeared on the screen. Bolan typed in *Scandinavian terrorist,* pushed the Enter button and watched as the list shortened to eight names. He typed in *code name and/or alias?,* hit the Enter button and watched as six of the names evaporated. He typed the words *associated with Dag Vaino and/or Franzen Stensvik and/or North Haakovia.*

"Colonel?"

One of the remaining two names disappeared and the Executioner stared at the screen. *Eremar, Sture Lars* remained. Under the alias, the words *Real Name: Selin, Sigrid Kuhmo.* Bolan typed in *photo available?*

The picture of a Finn with longish blond hair and a small white scar on his left cheek appeared on the monitor. The Executioner hit the "print" button and a photocopy of the picture rolled out of the printer.

"Colonel Pollock, are you there?"

Bolan ripped the copy from the tray. Swiveling in his chair, he turned to the copy machine, shoved it under the cover and pressed the green button. "I'm here," he said into the radio.

"Repeat," came the voice on the other end of the walkie-talkie. "We have no idea what this man looks like, Colonel."

Bolan stared at the tray as copy after copy of Selin's picture came rolling out. In the distance the explosions still rocked the castle walls as Stensvik's North Haakovian air force bombed its way toward Larsborg. He glanced toward the wall.

On the other side of the stone was another bomb, a bomb that might take out the whole floor at any moment.

The Executioner tore the photocopies out of the tray and swung open the door to the hall as the walkie-talkie scratched again. "Colonel Pollock, we don't know—"

Bolan cut him off. "Meet me at the stairs," he ordered the castle security chief. "You'll know what he looks like then."

YAKOV KATZENELENBOGEN had seen better jails in his time. Then again, he'd seen much worse.

The bars, combination sink-toilet and metal bunks had all been painted a dull institutional green. The dirty blue-and-white-striped mattress on which he lay had no sheets, and the blanket he had been issued threatened to fall apart if even one more cigarette butt was put out in its fabric.

The concrete walls—green like the bars—were covered with obscene sketches of male and female genitalia, and what Katz assumed to be obscene Finnish poetry. The mixed odor of sweat, cigarette smoke and stale urine permeated the air.

No, it wasn't the Beverly Hills lockup by any means. On the other hand, he was being treated considerably better than he would be were he imprisoned in Baghdad or Tripoli.

Katz folded his arms behind his head and stretched his legs on the top bunk, staring at the ceiling. The men of Phoenix Force had been separated immediately upon arrest, even being transported to the holding facility in different vehicles. They had seen one another briefly in the main office, then been segregated again, not only in different cells, but in different "runs," and for all Katz knew, on different floors.

Beneath him, Katz heard the click of a cigarette lighter. Smoke began to rise past him toward the ceiling. In a moment now, he knew the man on the bottom bunk would offer him a smoke.

And Katz would accept. The Finnish police had taken his Camels. Along with his money, weapons and prosthetic arm.

The Phoenix Force leader rubbed his left hand over the stub on the other side of his body. He wondered if they'd found the hidden .22 Magnum pistol within the fake limb. If not, he might be able to talk them into—

The metal shrieked slightly as the man on the bottom bunk rose to a sitting position. Katz peered over the edge of the filthy mattress and saw a long nose, pinched face and stringy dishwater-blond hair looking up at him. The man's narrow lips twisted into a smile as he lifted a pack of Danish E. Noble Petits, and said something in Finnish.

Katz fought a grin. It was all too predictable.

The thin lips switched to Swedish, then Haakovian, and finally Danish before finally saying, "English?"

The Israeli nodded. "Or French."

"You will take a cigarette?" the man asked, shaking one from the pack.

Katz nodded, stuck it in his mouth and let the man light it with a cheap disposable lighter.

A bony hand stretched up. "I am Karl. And you are?"

"Samuel," Katz replied. "Call me Sam." He inhaled a lung full of smoke. Next would come the query regarding his imprisonment.

"Ah, Sam," the man said. "Tell me. Why have they arrested you?"

Katz shrugged. "They think I am a terrorist."

The narrow eyes on the bottom bunk narrowed even more. The man glanced dramatically over his shoulder through the bars to the empty run. He turned back, then stood and rested his elbows on the top bunk.

Katz sat up to give him room, and rested his back against the wall.

Karl leaned in closer to whisper. When he did, his shirt stretched across his back, and Katz saw the outline of the wire he'd known would be there.

The Phoenix Force leader didn't know whether Karl was an undercover cop or just a jail-house snitch. But whichever he was, he didn't know his work as well as he should have.

"You are with Vaino?" Karl asked softly.

The man staring innocently into Katz's eyes was twenty, maybe twenty-two years old, tops. Which meant that the former Israeli Mossad agent had been playing games like this before Karl was born. Katz took another drag on the cigarette. "No," he said. "I don't know anyone named Vaino."

The cop smiled slyly. "No, of course you don't." He glanced over his shoulder again for effect, then turned back. "Neither do *I.*"

"They think you're a terrorist, too?" Katz said, playing along.

Karl nodded, grinning. "But *of course* they are wrong."

Katz laughed. "Of course."

"Vaino will free us," Karl whispered. "You will see."

Katz nodded. "Well, that would be nice. If he does, tell him I owe him one . . . whoever the hell he is."

The cop frowned. He opened his mouth to speak again, then stopped as the clink of a heavy metal key being inserted into the door at the end of the run echoed through the cell. The wire beneath the man's shirt was attached to a transmitter, allowing other cops to monitor what was said in the cell. Karl might not have given up yet.

But whoever was in charge of this charade had.

The Israeli rolled to the edge of the bed as the barred door swung open. A thin man dressed in the blue uniform of the Finnish police led another man, taller and heavyset, into the cell. The heavyset man wore a brown Finnish army uniform with colonel's bars on the epaulets. A matching brown service-dress peaked cap covered his head.

"You will come with us," the colonel said flatly.

Katz scooted off the edge of the bunk, dropped the remainder of his cigarette to the floor and crushed it under his boot. The Finnish officers each grabbed an arm and ushered him from the cell and down the run.

A minute later, the Phoenix Force leader found himself in an interrogation room. The walls were soundproofed with thick shag carpet. A mirror was positioned just to the side of the door—a one-way mirror, Katz knew.

The cop nodded to the colonel, then left.

Katz knew what that meant, and he wasn't surprised. The cops had had enough of the assassinations and terrorist attacks. They were washing their hands of the situation, handing it over to the army.

The colonel indicated a chair at the table in the center of the room. Katz took a seat. The burly man took the chair across from him and fished a pack of Muratti Ambassadors and a box of matches from the breast pocket of his blouse. He placed them on the table and gestured toward them with a hand.

Katz took one of the Swiss cigarettes and lighted it with a match. He inhaled deeply, letting the smoke trail out the corners of his mouth.

"I am Colonel Mallaskatu."

The Israeli remained silent.

"Your name?" Mallaskatu demanded.

Katz provided the name under which he'd checked into the Grand Hotel. "Wilenzick," he replied. "Samuel Wilenzick."

"You are Jewish?"

Katz nodded.

"What are you doing in Helsinki?"

There was little sense in telling the colonel that he and the rest of Phoenix Force were here on a sightseeing tour. They'd been arrested with enough weaponry to start a small war, which was exactly what Mallaskatu thought they'd been doing.

No, it made more sense to try to level with the colonel. At least as much as possible. Maybe Mallaskatu would see that they were his allies, not his enemies.

"We are here to help you," the Israeli said.

The colonel's beefy fist rose in the air and slammed down into the metal table, sounding like two orchestra cymbals colliding within the small interrogation room. "You are lying," he gritted between clenched teeth. "You and your men are terrorists. In the employee of Dag Vaino."

Katz shook his head. "You're wrong," he replied, staring the man in the eyes.

Mallaskatu met his stare. His fist rose again, but this time the broad knuckles drove into Katz's face. The Israeli flipped backward in his chair and landed on the cold concrete floor. The coppery taste of blood filled his mouth, and when he looked up, he saw *two* Finnish colonels standing over him.

"You are lying!" the double vision shouted. He drew back a boot and kicked Katz in the ribs.

The Phoenix Force leader heard a crack. He rolled to his side, his arm moving protectively to the injured ribs as flames shot through his torso. The next thing he knew, he was being hauled to his feet and thrown back into the chair.

"You and your men have already been identified by officers who were outside city hall this morning. We know you took part in the assassination of Risto

Kalle." Mallaskatu paused, drew in a breath, then continued. "I will ask you again. What is your next planned act of terrorism in Finland?"

As his vision began to clear, Katz shook his head. "You're wrong," he repeated. The big fist flashed before his face, and he found himself once more on the floor.

Again, Mallaskatu hauled him into the chair. The big colonel leaned down and pressed his face into Katz's. "If you do not confess and alert us to what is planned next, you and your comrades will be executed immediately." He stood up and folded his arms across his chest.

Blood dribbled from the corner of Katz's mouth when he spoke. "We have had no trial," he said. "When did Finland become a barbaric dictatorship in which men are summarily executed with no opportunity to defend themselves?"

A wicked grin broke out on Mallaskatu's face. "The situation is unusual, I grant you. But rest assured, it is possible. Now, for the final time, do you wish to speak?"

Katz said nothing. He closed his eyes as the heavy fist pummelled him to the concrete once more. From the floor, he heard a buzzer sound. He opened his eyes, noting that the left brow had now swollen down over the socket. He heard the key in the door and rolled to his side to see the police lieutenant standing next to the table.

Mallaskatu reached down and grabbed the collar of his shirt. The big man half carried him down the run to a larger room. The police officer opened the door, and the Finnish colonel threw him inside.

Katz landed on his belly. Almost immediately he felt more hands trying to raise him to his feet. When he opened his good eye, he saw Calvin James staring down at him. The tissue around James's eyes was swollen, similar to his own.

Rafael Encizo and Gary Manning pulled Katz from the floor to his feet. The Israeli wobbled on uncertain legs as they braced him on both sides. If their faces were any indication, both Encizo and Manning had gone through interrogations similar to his and James's.

Fire shot through the Israeli's ribs and face, but as his good eye continued to clear, he saw something that pushed the pain into the recesses of his mind and lightened his heart.

Standing just behind Manning, James and Encizo was a familiar figure.

"Bloody can't believe it," David McCarter said, shaking his head. "I let you blokes out of my sight for half a minute, and just look what happens to you."

3

Able Team reached Harmony Cove in time to see the Grumman Mallard's pontoons skid across the water and rise into the air. Facing away from the Stony Man warriors, the Colombian and both Haakovians stood on the deck of the submarine, watching the plane take off.

The dark-skinned man died to the tune of Gadgets Schwarz's sound-suppressed Uzi, the silver toes of the Colombian's boots flashing under the sun as he plummeted headfirst into the water. The Haakovians turned toward the strange coughing sound. Blancanales cut a figure eight back and forth between the pair, and they slumped to the deck.

Lyons held back, letting the men with the silenced weapons handle the job. For all he knew, the crate to which Bolan had attached the tracking device had been unloaded, and if Able Team didn't reach the hatch before the Mike submerged again, there was no telling where the chemicals on board would end up.

Able Team sprinted toward the water. As they passed the trees, Turrin broke from cover to join the race, a Smith & Wesson Model 66 extended from his left hand. The little Fed had swung the MAC-10 formerly hidden by his suit coat to the end of the sling, and held its pistol grip in his other fist. "I tried to raise you," he puffed between breaths, "but—"

Lyons cut him off with a wave of the hand. He tapped the wire leading from his headset as they ran on. "They hear anything?" he whispered.

Turrin shook his head. "Don't think so. But they've already loaded the plane. It left."

"We saw."

The four Stony Man warriors hit the water and began sloshing toward the Mike. Thirty feet from the deck, they hit deeper water and swam silently on.

Schwarz was the first to reach the top of the sub. He pulled himself up over the side and rolled to a squatting position. Water dripped from his Uzi as he aimed the weapon down into the open hatch. Lyons, Blancanales and Turrin followed him on board.

"Able One to Birdman," Lyons whispered. "Come in, Charlie."

The radio crackled in his ear. "Mott here."

"You see the Mallard just took off?" he said.

"I saw it."

"Go after it, Charlie. Don't lose it. They've got chemical nerve agents on board."

Mott whistled. In the background Lyons heard him rev the engine of the Cessna 421 that had brought them to Key West. "On my way," the pilot said. "Haven't hunted mallards for some time now."

The men of Able Team moved closer to the hatch, and Lyons lowered his voice even further. "Right," he said. "But don't engage in any duck shooting, Charlie. You rupture the canister, and that stuff might spread in the wind. Just see where they're going and make sure they don't spot you. We'll grab a lift with the first

Delta unit that arrives and catch up to you." He let up on the key.

Lyons glanced up briefly and saw the Cessna rise into the air and take off after the Mallard.

The men from Stony Man Farm stopped at the hatch. Lyons turned to face them. "I'll go down first," he said. "Come after me, one at a time."

Lyons dropped to his belly and peered into the opening. His knowledge of submarines, especially Soviet subs, was about equal to his expertise in the mating habits of Tokay geckos. But he did recognize an engine room when he saw one.

A man in the gaudy blue-and-red uniform of the North Haakovian navy stood facing away from the hatch. He twisted one of the dozens of dials in front of him, and the engines purred louder.

The vessel was preparing to submerge.

Rising to his knees, Lyons stuck the .45 through the hatch and pulled the trigger. The bullet caught the Haakovian between the shoulder blades, folding him in half and sending him crashing into the engines.

Lyons dropped into the engine room in a crouch, swinging the .45 through a full 360-degree turn. Two passageways led from the engine room. A ladder disappeared to the level below. Satisfied that there was no one else in the room, the Able Team leader stuck his head through the hatch and nodded.

The other three men lowered themselves into the Mike.

As soon as they were down, Lyons whispered, "Leo, you and Pol watch the passageways. We're damn lucky there was no one else in here, but that luck can't last forever."

Turrin and Blancanales moved toward the passageways.

Lyons kept one eye on the ladder as he turned to Schwarz. "What's the best way to screw this thing up, Gadgets?" he asked.

Schwarz frowned at the machinery in front of him. "You want something easy or something complicated?"

"I want something fast."

The electronics wizard's frown became a smile. "Then we'll sink it." Moving to the dials, the frown returned as he studied them, then began twisting, turning and flipping switches.

Lyons heard the screech of heavy gears grinding come from various parts of the sub, and the sound of excited voices came from both passageways.

Schwarz turned more dials and a dull thud sounded in the engines. He raised his Uzi, flipped the selector to semiauto and quickly circled the machines, putting a bullet into the face of each dial. When he'd finished, he hurried across the room to another control panel.

"What are you doing now?" Lyons asked.

"I just screwed the engines up to the point that they won't be leaving without a major overhaul," he said. "We're about to drop down a few feet. So I'd say it's time to open the rest of the hatches."

Footsteps pounded down the passageways as Gadgets began fiddling with the controls. Lyons turned back to the ladder as he heard a hatch slide open somewhere close by. To his left he saw three men in blue and red screech to a halt as they reached the end of the passageway.

Blancanales opened fire, and the North Haakovians collapsed to the floor of the vessel.

A head appeared at the top of the steps. Lyons pumped a .45 slug into it, then turned as Leo Turrin opened fire with his MAC-10, slicing through the chest of a Haakovian seaman who had tried to enter the engine room through the passageway the undercover man was guarding.

Lyons felt a hand on his sleeve. "The sub's going down," Schwarz told him. "So I'd suggest *we* go up."

A foot of water already covered the deck by the time the Stony Man warriors pulled themselves through the hatch. They dived off the sides, swam to shore and started back through the trees.

Lyons tapped the radio button again as they broke into a jog. "Able to Base."

"Stony Man here," Barbara Price came back.

"Any word on the Delta boys?"

Before Price could answer, the sound of aircraft engines suddenly roared above. Lyons looked up to see two T-tailed de Havilland Caribous heading toward the runway where Mott had just taken off. "They're here, Barb."

Lyons, and the other three men quickened their pace. They found Turrin's Lincoln Mark IV hidden in the trees where they'd left it. As Schwarz and Blancanales jerked the branches from the hood and roof, the big ex-cop radioed again. "There's something else I need, Stony."

"Name it."

"I don't know what we're going to do once we catch the seaplane. We can't shoot it down without taking the chance that the nerve agents will be blown all over the Greater Antilles. Sarin and soman are both older chemicals. They're persistent. Ask Bear to run this situation through his computers, figure all the angles and probabilities, and then have a counterterrorist equipment package put together for us at the nearest military base."

Kurtzman's voice came over the air. "I heard, Ironman, and I'm on my way. Keep us informed as to your location."

"That's affirmative," Lyons said. He jumped into the Lincoln's shotgun seat. Turrin slid behind the wheel, and Schwarz and Blancanales jumped in back. Sand and dirt shot from the car's rear tires as they headed down the road toward the landing strip.

Lyons killed the satellite relay and switched the radio to a military frequency. "Come in, Delta," he said.

"Captain Norton here," a gravelly Southern voice came back. "You got a sub down here needs to be baby-sat?"

"That's affirmative," Lyons said. "You guys bring your snorkels?"

"Imagine we can round up a few."

"Good." Lyons ran down the situation with the sub and seaplane, then gave Norton directions to Harmony Cove and told him about the chemicals in the two pickups. "Get some men on the way," he said. "But keep a pilot there for us. We've got a plane to catch."

Turrin pulled around a curve and the landing strip appeared. The undercover ace screeched to a halt next to the nearest Caribou. A jeep full of Delta Force commandos came chugging through the double cargo door before squealing away toward Harmony Cove.

Lyons jumped out in front of a tall angular man dressed in OD-green fatigues and floppy bush hat. Like the other men of Delta Force, he carried an Army-issued M-16A2 slung over his shoulder, but his side arm was personalized—a 10 mm Colt Delta Elite.

The man stepped forward and extended his hand. "Reb Norton," he said.

Lyons grasped the hand. "Let's get going." He turned toward Turrin, then pointed to the jeep kicking up dust clouds toward Harmony Cove.

"Go back with them, Leo," he said. "Make sure they find everything."

Turrin nodded. The Mark IV took off after the jeep.

Norton led Able Team into the Caribou and took a seat behind the controls. As they started down the runway, Lyons keyed the mike on his radio. "Able One to Birdman."

"The Bird's got ears," Mott came back. "Come at me, Ironman."

"Location?"

"Southeast of Andros," Mott said. "Nearing the Ragged Island Range."

"Any idea yet where they're headed?"

"Negative, Ironman. They're keeping a steady course, but there's a thousand possibilities along this route."

"Roger, Charlie. They spotted you?"

"Don't think so. But there's no way to be sure. You boys in the air yet?"

The Caribou hit the end of the runway and took off over the clear blue water. "Affirmative, Birdman," Lyons said. "We're on your tail."

The ex-LAPD detective settled back into his seat for what was usually the hard part of any mission. Waiting. At this point, everything was being done that could be done. Turrin and the Delta Force commandos should have reached Harmony Cove by now and secured the pickups. Barbara Price would have notified the U.S. Navy, and by now a fleet of American vessels would be en route to converge on the Soviet Mike and whatever might remain in the hold.

And Kurtzman was putting together a counterterrorist equipment package for Able Team to use when they finally caught up to the Grumman Mallard.

Waiting, Lyons thought again. Yeah, usually that was the hard part. But this time, he had plenty to do while he waited. Like trying to figure out just how Able Team could neutralize the seaplane without contaminating the entire Caribbean.

Lyons's brows lowered in concentration as the Caribou gained altitude. This deal had another aspect, one he'd put off dealing with so far. Leaving Key West meant that Able Team was no longer in U.S. territory. And the President had been clear in his orders not to work outside their sanction. The ex-cop felt his fingers curl over the edge of the seat. He wasn't a man who liked violating the orders of his leader, but dammit, right was right and wrong was wrong. And no matter where wrong took place, Carl Lyons felt an inner drive—no, a need—to do what he could to stop it.

And he would.

Lyons flipped the mike into his hand again and keyed it. "Able One to Stony Man."

"Come in," Price came back.

He ran down the situation. "See if Hal can get the Man on the phone and get us permission to fire outside U.S. territory."

"Roger. But that could take awhile to get through channels."

"I know," Lyons replied, trying to keep the irritation out of his voice. "That's why I'm starting the red tape early." He hung the mike up, sat back and took a deep breath.

Yeah. Right was right, and wrong was wrong, and never the twain would meet. There was no telling how many innocent people would die if the chemicals on board the Grumman got into the wrong hands.

Lyons knew what he would do if it became necessary.

With, or without, the sanction of the President.

DEEP IN THE HEART of the Shenandoah Valley, just below Stony Man Mountain where for four years Confederate General Stonewall Jackson humiliated Union forces during the American Civil War, lies an innocuous-looking little agrobusiness known as Stony Man Farm.

From the road, motorists can see a landing strip within the carefully cultivated fields. A tractor barn, and several outbuildings sit near the main house in the center of the tract, which looks little different than the homes of other wealthy farmers in the valley.

Among other crops, Stony Man Farm produces cotton. It even shows a profit at the end of every year, and the Farm pays the appropriate income taxes on that profit. But unlike most American businesses, the administrators of Stony Man foster no resentment toward the IRS. They know that what they contribute to the American tax system, and more, will be returned to them at the end of every fiscal year so that they might continue to operate the other, chief function of the Farm: protecting the United States of America from communism, authoritarianism, terrorism and organized crime.

Few Americans know what Stony Man Farm's real function is. Those who do all play a direct part in its operation. They are the men of Phoenix Force and Able Team, the two top counterterrorist commando squads in the world; the other, lesser-known units and specialists who stand ready to give their expertise—and if need be their very lives—to ensure that America remains free; and the office and technical staff that live and work at the Farm, men and women most often drawn from the military, law enforcement, or other branches of the government because of their technological proficiency.

Mack Bolan, also known as the Executioner, was once a full-time member of the Stony Man team. He still keeps an arm's-length relationship with the Farm while waging his one-man war against evil the world over.

For all practical purposes, the Executioner answers to no one. He never has. He never will. But his living legend remains the heart, soul and inspiration of Stony Man Farm.

Hal Brognola, a high-ranking official within the U.S. Department of Justice, is Stony Man Farm's Director of Sensitive Operations. Unlike Bolan, he does answer to one man.

The Man.

The President of the United States of America.

ON TOP OF HIS RAMP in the computer room on the first floor of the main house, Aaron Kurtzman leaned against the back of his wheelchair and studied the beeping dot on the color monitor in front of him. A tight knot had formed in his abdomen the moment Lyons notified Stony Man Farm of the cargo carried by the Soviet submarine.

Sarin and soman. The two gases weren't simply biochemical nerve agents, they were old biochemical nerve agents. They were hell to control, and dammit, once they got loose, they didn't dissipate soon.

The sub might have been neutralized, but the knot in his stomach hadn't. The plane, and the fact that the sarin and soman were being distributed all over Europe and the Americas, was enough to keep the knot firmly in place.

Looking back at the monitor, Kurtzman hit the "exit" button and wiped away the link to U.S. naval command. He had been in the process of establishing contact with American nuclear subs in case the Mike got away from Able Team.

Thank God it hadn't. There would have been a nuclear Mexican standoff the likes of which the world hadn't seen since the Cuban missile crisis.

"Okay," Kurtzman said out loud as his fingers began to fly across the keys again, "the sub's down. But there's plenty of other work to do." With the finesse of a concert pianist, his hands played the keyboard, accessing the probability program he had recently created and installed himself. A menu appeared on the screen. He hit the number 1 for *Situation*, and the words *Enter Details* appeared. Hurriedly the computer wizard typed in the particulars of Able Team's predicament with the seaplane, then hit Enter again.

Clicks sounded within the hardware as it digested the information. The menu reappeared. Kurtzman pressed 2 for *Location*, then typed *Greater Antilles Area*. Number 4 accessed him to *Probable Scenarios*, and 5 brought up *Equipment Preferred*. He responded accordingly.

The information entered, Kurtzman cleared the screen again and accessed the portion of his program he'd entitled "Analysis." He typed in *Evaluate situation and provide equipment list*, and the computer clicked again.

Kurtzman frowned in concentration. He added *Provide location of nearest U.S. military installation able to provide equipment*, then sat back.

Stony Man's computer genius lifted the Wellington briar pipe from the stand next to the monitor and stuck it between his lips. He wished momentarily for tobacco and a light, then pushed the thought from his mind. The computers at Stony Man were worth millions, and the American taxpayer didn't need to replace them just because Aaron Kurtzman wanted to indulge his vice. But there was another reason Kurtzman never smoked in the computer room, a reason far more important than money.

The lives of Mack Bolan, the men of Able Team and Phoenix Force, and the rest of the Stony Man crew often depended on how quickly his machines could provide them with the information they needed. And Kurtzman had no intention of causing their deaths because he needed a smoke.

The phone buzzed in the communications room and Kurtzman turned to look through the glass divider. Barbara Price lifted the receiver to her ear with one hand and drew a pencil from the holder on her console with the other. Kurtzman watched her scribble furiously on a notepad, then lean forward on the microphone key and speak into the instrument.

A beep sounded in front of him and Kurtzman turned back to the task at hand. A long list of equipment appeared on the screen. Beneath the list appeared the words: *Nearest U.S. Military Base Containing All Items: Roosevelt Roades Naval Base, San Juan Puerto Rico.*

Kurtzman studied the suggested equipment, and a smile formed on his lips. Some of the articles looked like they belonged on a Christmas list for some spoiled rich kid.

Kurtzman pushed the "print" button, then transferred the job from his printer to Price's in the next room. He watched through the glass as the page came rolling out of the machine. Price picked it up, glanced at it, then lifted her phone. A second later, his intercom buzzed.

"You sure about some of this stuff, Aaron?"

"The machines don't lie."

"Okay. I'll get in touch with Rosie Roades and have them put it all together." Price paused. When she spoke again, her voice had lowered to an almost-reverent whisper. "This is going to be thin, Bear. *Real* thin. I hope to hell we see these guys again."

"So do I, Barb. So do I."

THE FACE IN THE MIRROR wasn't what Franzen Stensvik would have chosen had he been given the choice. The large Slavic head appeared dwarflike on top of his narrow frame. The extra shoulder padding Anton had added to the jacket hadn't helped. And the deep pockmarks left over from his teenage battle with acne showed through the makeup applied by the woman he had expropriated from the Russian ballet company stationed in Sturegorsk.

Stensvik frowned. The cratered skin made him look like that fool Manuel Noriega. His lips curled into a snarl. He would give the makeup artist one more chance, and if she didn't find a way to cover the scars, he would see to it that his face looked like a baby's compared to hers.

Stensvik continued to stare into the mirror. The makeup artist still on his mind, a cruel pleasure suddenly filled his heart. No, he wasn't handsome. But like so many other powerful men throughout history, his substandard appearance hadn't stopped his conquest of the females he desired. The North Haakovian president's snarl turned to a smile. The women who hadn't shared his bed willingly had shared it through force.

Sex was like everything else in life for the man who had power. You took what you wanted, whether others wanted you to have it or not. And many times, it was more fun to take than to be given.

"Hat," Stensvik said, raising his hand. He didn't bother to look over his shoulder, knowing full well that Anton would press the carefully cleaned cap into his fingers. Anton Danielovitch knew what the consequences would be if he didn't adhere to his master's every whim. Like the makeup artist, the frail little man with the delicate features had come from the Russian ballet, where he had been in charge of costuming.

The president placed the hat on top of his head. He frowned again as he continued to study his appearance in the mirror. Behind him, he saw Anton watching him. When he met the man's eye, the costumer turned away.

Stensvik smoothed his sleeves and straightened his jacket. Anton had helped him design his vestment, which was actually a combination of several uniforms. The hat, shoulder boards and collar tabs were red copies of the green that had been worn by the now-defunct Soviet border guards.

"Belt," Stensvik said. Anton handed it to him, and he slipped into it. The shiny white leather garrison belt had been inspired by the British Royal Military Police. The spit-shined jackboots had come from pictures of Hitler's Third Reich, and the white spats over the boots had been Stensvik's own idea.

He continued to stare. The holstered gun on his side made his uniform sag. Unsnapping the flap, he drew the gold-plated Crvena Zastava Model 83 and handed it to Anton. "Carry it for me."

Anton took the Yugoslavian .357 Magnum revolver.

"Whip," Stensvik said, and was passed the riding crop.

Stensvik stood at attention, then slapped the short whip against his thigh with a resounding pop. The sound brought a genuine smile to his face. It recalled his final pleasure with a number of women who had avoided his advances. With a last glance into the glass, he turned on his heel and headed to the door, pausing while Anton opened it. He strode through the opening into the hall, his boots clicking down the tile, pleased when he heard Anton's own footsteps hurrying to keep pace behind him.

A dozen men wearing gold-braided honor-brigade uniforms and clutching AK-74 assault rifles stood along the hallway. They fell into place behind their leader as he passed. A man in civilian attire, carrying a camera bag, fell in as well.

Two more soldiers opened the door to the front of the newly constructed prefab government building, and another four formed a protective cocoon around Stensvik as he strode toward the limousine waiting at the curb. Anton opened the rear door of the vehicle. Stensvik slid inside and watched his valet round the limo and get in next to him as the soldiers piled into cars in front and behind.

Five minutes later, they pulled to a halt in front of the Hotel Svendborg. Anton opened his door and Stensvik stepped out onto the pavement. Sauntering past the sidewalk terrace, the North Haakovian president mounted the steps past the aristocratic pillars and entered the spacious lobby, the thrill of what he was about to do flowing through his veins.

America would pay for its insolence and lack of respect.

Stensvik marched to the elevators and waited while Anton pressed the call button. In his peripheral vision he saw a bearded form in a tuxedo approach. He turned to face the man.

The hotel manager bowed his head. "Mr. President," he said. "Had we known you were coming, we would have prepared—"

Stensvik cut him off with a cough. "Where is your best banquet room?" he demanded.

The manager kept his head down. "On the mezzanine."

"How is the lighting?"

The manager glanced up. "Sir?"

Stensvik blew air through his teeth in irritation. "The lighting, dammit! How is the lighting for photographs?"

The manager's eyes returned to his shoes. "The lighting is excellent, Mr. President. But at the moment, the room is occupied by—"

"Clear it," Stensvik said as the elevator doors opened. He stepped inside, followed by his entourage. Anton pressed the button for the fourth floor, and Stensvik's smile returned as the car ascended the shaft.

Yes, America would pay for what it had done. He had decided so last night. It had become apparent that his bid for a seat at the United Nations was futile at this moment in history, and while that had been a disappointment in some ways, in many others it had come as a relief. With nothing left to lose, it had freed him to attack the bitch who now ran South Haakovia. And to get his revenge upon the United States, which he held responsible for the unsuccessful attempt at the UN.

The elevator doors opened and Stensvik stepped out. He stalked down the hall until the numerals 408 appeared on a door to his right. Turning, he lifted a boot and sent it crashing into the wood.

The door swung open.

Stensvik stepped back as half a dozen soldiers rushed in. They appeared a moment later dragging Walter Jacobson, the American ambassador to North Haakovia. Overweight and clad only in boxer shorts and a white ribbed undershirt, shaving cream covered half of Jacobson's face.

"Get him cleaned and dressed, you fools!" Stensvik shouted. The men dragged Jacobson back into the room. The president turned to the other soldiers. "How many aides does he have?"

"Three."

"Get them."

Half a dozen soldiers in honor-guard uniforms hurried down the hall, kicking in the doors and dragging protesting Americans from their rooms.

Stensvik waited. Five minutes later, Walter Jacobson reappeared dressed in a navy suit. Soldiers held both of his arms.

"What is the meaning of this?" Jacobson demanded. "You cannot—"

Stensvik slapped him across the face. "Silence!" he roared. He turned and strode back to the elevator, the others falling in behind him like faithful dogs.

A moment later they entered the banquet room and Stensvik was irritated to see that while the room had been cleared of people, the remnants of the breakfast that had been in progress still remained on the long tables. He made a mental note. "Line them up," he ordered his men.

The soldiers pushed Jacobson and his aides against the wall.

"What in hell do you think you're—"

One of the soldiers punched Jacobson in the stomach. He dropped to his knees, choking. His eyes bulged and his face filled with color.

The soldiers jerked him back to his feet.

Stensvik handed the riding crop over his shoulder and felt Anton take it. He left his hand there, and said, "File."

The valet pressed a manila folder into his fingers.

Stensvik opened the file and began reading. "For war crimes against the people of North Haakovia—"

Jacobson regained his breath. "What? War crimes! What—"

Another fist silenced him.

The president went on as if nothing had happened. "For war crimes against the people of North Haakovia," he repeated, "I sentence you to death. Sentence to be carried out immediately."

One of the aides spoke up. "But we have committed no crimes!"

Another of the frightened men stepped forward. "No, President Stensvik . . . please . . ."

Jacobson caught his breath again. "You can't do this," he said desperately.

"Gun!" Stensvik shouted.

Anton handed him the gold-plated .357 Magnum.

Stensvik swung the cylinder out, checked the load, then swung it back into the revolver. Nodding to the photographer, he stepped in front of the American at the end of the line and pressed the golden barrel against the man's temple.

"Stensvik! You can't—" Jacobson screamed.

The president pulled the trigger. The explosion drowned out the rest of the American ambassador's words.

The man in front of Franzen Stensvik slumped to the floor as blood and brains sprayed the wallpaper. The rest of the Americans stood frozen in place, staring down at the horror at their feet.

Stensvik moved to the next man in line, shoving the revolver into his mouth and pulling the trigger. The back of the American's head exploded.

The North Haakovian president curiously watched the pattern the man's blood made on the wallpaper. He snickered, then moved to the aide next to Jacobson and rested the gun on the bridge of the man's nose.

A sudden impulse caught him, and Stensvik lowered the weapon to the man's genitals. He saw the terror in the American's eyes, and felt a warm surge of excitement in his lower abdomen.

He fired.

The American's bottom lip dropped in shock. He screamed and fell to his knees, his hands clasped together on his crotch as he jerked convulsively.

Stensvik laughed. The warmth in his belly moved lower, and he felt a tingle in his scrotum. An erection began, and as it grew, he pressed the golden barrel of the .357 against the top of the weeping man's head and fired again.

The American quit jerking.

Jacobson screamed and bolted toward the door. Two of the soldiers caught the chubby ambassador by the arms and lifted him into the air. They carried him back, kicking and flailing, and slammed him against the wall.

Stensvik stepped in close and stabbed the revolver into the man's throat.

"But, but, but," Jacobson babbled almost incoherently. His eyes darted back and forth across the room, looking for help. "You can't!" he screamed. "I have a wife! Children!"

"Is your wife here in Sturegorsk?" Stensvik asked.

Jacobson's quivering mouth suddenly clamped shut.

"She is," Anton replied.

"Good." Stensvik smiled, turning toward the soldiers. "Have her brought to my bedroom when we return."

"No!" Jacobson screamed again. "You can't...we have...we have *your* representatives in Washington! The United States will retaliate!"

Stensvik cocked the revolver. "Don't be ridiculous. When was the last time you heard of the United States doing something this barbaric?"

Jacobson opened his mouth to speak again. When he did, Stensvik shoved the barrel past his teeth until it stopped at the back of his throat. The explosion drowned out whatever the American's final words would have been.

Stensvik turned to the photographer. He pointed to the bodies on the floor with the gun, then transferred the weapon to his left hand and straightened his jacket. He pulled his hat a little lower to hide the scars on his forehead, then slipped his right hand inside his lapel and posed as the camera clicked away.

As the final picture flashed, Stensvik's eyes fell again on the breakfast remnants on the table. The manager had shown him great disrespect by not having the room cleaned. He turned to the photographer. "Have the pictures developed and send a set to the White House," he said. He opened the golden revolver's cylinder and extracted the five spent casings.

One round remained.

Turning to his soldiers, Stensvik said, "Bring me the hotel manager."

4

The Executioner met the captain of the castle guard halfway up the landing.

The castle walls shook harder as the aerial bombing drew closer to the capital. Bolan shoved the Photostat pictures into the captain's hand. "Get them distributed," he ordered. "I want the castle searched with a fine-tooth comb. The man's name is Sigrid Selin. The picture doesn't show it, but tell your men he's wearing a mustache." Bolan paused. "Selin's got a remote control that can set off the bomb in the chapel. He'll use it as soon as he's free, or if he thinks he's trapped. Shoot him on sight. No questions. No hesitation."

The captain nodded and disappeared down the steps.

Bolan cleared his mind, then imagined what he'd do if he was in Selin's shoes.

Okay. The mass of people being herded downstairs would have alerted Selin that his plan had gone awry. But if he'd been trained by Dag Vaino, Selin would have a backup plan.

What?

The warrior closed his eyes, the muscles in his face tensing. The explosion would be set to go up. Would

Selin therefore go down? No, if he had any brains at all, he'd know the exits would be sealed immediately.

Selin would have to go up, in spite of the bomb.

The Executioner pivoted and started up the steps three at a time. He grabbed the rail of the fourth-floor landing with his left hand, pulling himself around the corner as his right drew the Desert Eagle. His eyes flickered back and forth as he reached the fifth floor, fully aware that Selin could be hiding around the corner in ambush. He glanced up, and thought he saw movement in the stairwell above him. Then a cool breeze drifted down the steps and across his face. The sound of a door being softly closed met his ears.

Someone had just closed the door to the castle roof.

Bolan bounded up the final flight of stairs, the big .44 Magnum pressed close to his side. When he reached the door he stopped, pressing an ear against the ancient wood.

Footsteps padded softly across the roof outside. Then another bomb fell somewhere to the north, masking the sound.

The Executioner ripped the door open, dived through the opening and fell into a shoulder roll. He came to his feet in a combat stance next to one of several antiaircraft guns mounted on the roof.

Selin stood less than ten feet away, looking up.

The hacking sound of rotor blades met the Executioner's ears, and he saw the helicopter above the terrorist. The red hammer-sickle-and-fish insignia of North Haakovia flashed into view as the aircraft prepared to land.

Selin turned toward the Executioner, his lips curling in a profane grin. His hand darted inside his coat, fumbling into an inner pocket.

Bolan dropped the Desert Eagle's sights on the terrorist's chest as Selin started to pull his hand from his pocket. But as the big pistol's trigger moved back, a sudden volley of .50-caliber machine-gun fire erupted from the helicopter, tearing at the tar around the Executioner's feet.

The warrior dived behind the antiaircraft gun, his shot flying high. As more fire pursued him from the chopper, he glanced at the heavy cannon mounted to the roof.

The barrel pointed the wrong way, and he had no time to disengage it and swing it around.

In one smooth, lightning movement, the Executioner dropped the box magazine of jacketed hollowpoint .44 Magnums from his weapon and shoved a clip of armor-piercing rounds into the well. Then he rose from cover and fired the hollowpoint still chambered toward the chopper.

The round hit the bubble, cracked the hard plastic, then ricocheted harmlessly off the shell.

The Desert Eagle's gas-operated three-lug bolt jacked an armor-piercer into the chamber.

Bolan dropped the .44's front post sight on the bubble of the helicopter, then aligned the dovetailed rear. Through the bullet-resistant plastic, he saw an expression of disbelief come over the face of the chopper's pilot.

The Executioner squeezed the trigger.

The big .44 drilled through the bubble and into the pilot's forehead. The look of disbelief on the man's face changed to one of shock.

The helicopter banked sharply, crashing into the edge of the roof. For what seemed like seconds the aircraft balanced as if riding a lopsided teeter-totter.

From the corner of his eye, Bolan saw Selin staring at the helicopter, his mouth agape. As the Executioner swung the big .44 toward the terrorist, the perching chopper suddenly burst into flames. A wall of fire swept across the tarry roof, forcing the warrior down.

Selin dived onto his belly, the remote-control detonator falling from his hand and bouncing to a halt a few feet away.

The flames from the explosion passed over Bolan's head, burning themselves out as quickly as they had ignited. The Executioner heard the screech of metal against stone as the chopper lost its purchase on the edge of the roof and slid down the outer wall of the castle. He vaulted back to his feet as the helicopter hit the ground and the secondary explosion sent more flames leaping up the stone walls.

Bolan swung the Desert Eagle back toward Selin as the man scrambled across the roof toward the detonator on hands and knees, his eyes gleaming with madness as he grasped the control in both hands.

The Executioner saw the tendons flex in the terrorist's wrists and Bolan squeezed the trigger.

The eruption from the chapel below sounded dull. The roof trembled, throwing the Executioner's shot high and to the right. He felt his legs give way as a wide fissure appeared in the tar halfway between him and Selin.

A moment later, he was rolling across the roof toward the terrorist.

Head over feet he tumbled as the fissure widened and the roof gave way. Then the Executioner's forehead cracked into Selin's as they rolled together in the middle of the roof.

As smoke rose through the air and flying debris struck his body, Bolan plummeted into the exploding castle, face-to-face with Sigrid Selin.

THE WHEELS of the heavy prison transport truck screeched as the vehicle pulled away from the holding facility and onto the streets of Helsinki.

Katz sat on the floor next to the rear door, his back pressed against the reinforced concrete wall. Next to him was Encizo, and on the other side of the little Cuban, Manning, James and McCarter.

Across from the men of Phoenix Force, their backs against the opposite wall, sat seven of Dag Vaino's terrorists. The men's hands were cuffed in front of them, and a heavy steel chain had been looped through the cuffs to link the men together.

Katz looked up to the barred window separating the prisoners from the cab of the paddy wagon. Through the glass, he could see the back of two heads—the police lieutenant and Colonel Mallaskatu. The two men faced forward, secure in the knowledge that their captives were well restrained.

The former Mossad agent glanced down the line to David McCarter. He and the rest of the team had been loaded into the transport vehicle just as the Briton had begun explaining what had happened to him in the South Harbor. The last he had told them was that he'd passed out under water.

Now, McCarter continued, whispering in a hushed voice. "So the next thing I know, I wake up and some foul, herring-breathed bloke has his mouth pressed against mine. It crossed my mind that I might have consumed a drop too much of a certain brown Scottish liquid, and passed out near a man whose sexual preferences differed considerably from my own."

Even amid the grim circumstances in which the men of Phoenix Force now found themselves, Katz couldn't suppress a smile.

"So," Manning said, "you decide to switch teams or what?"

McCarter snorted contemptuously. "Hardly. I rolled to my side and punched his nose for him."

"Doesn't appear it helped much," James commented, lifting his wrists. The chain clanked against the handcuffs. "You're here with us."

"No, it didn't help at all. The fact is, it got me a rifle butt in the lower abdomen and the next thing I knew I was regurgitating enough salt water to maintain a fairly good-size aquarium."

Katz chuckled along with the rest of the men. But beneath the light humor, he felt the tension. The men of Phoenix Force were waiting for him to come up with a plan to get them out of there, keep them alive and get on with the mission.

McCarter started to speak again, but a sharp rap on the cab window stopped him. Katz looked up to see Mallaskatu glaring back through the bars and holding a microphone to his lips.

The colonel's words echoed over the loudspeaker. "No talking," he ordered, first in Finnish, then in English.

Katz waited until the colonel turned around again, then lowered his voice to a whisper. "We'll have to get the rest of the details later, David. Right now, I think a little planning is in order." The Israeli's eyes flickered back to the bars. Only Mallaskatu and the Finnish cop were in front, but three jeeps, each carrying five soldiers, followed the prison wagon. Even if he and the rest of Phoenix Force were able to pick the lock on the rear door, even if they were able to jump from the speeding vehicle and survive the fall, they'd be shot dead before they quit rolling.

Not to mention the fact that they'd find themselves dragging seven of Vaino's terrorists by the chain.

Manning seemed to read his mind. "Anybody know exactly who they are?" the big Canadian asked, indicating the men across from them.

James shrugged. "I shared a cell with the one on the end," he said, nodding toward a bearded man who had a bleeding four-inch slash across his face. "They were captured a week or so ago on another deal."

Katz heard another rap on the glass. Mallaskatu glared between the bars, then turned around again. Katz lowered his voice further. "We're headed toward a firing squad."

McCarter nodded. "That's the general impression I get. Out of the South Harbor boiling pot, into the fire."

Encizo shook his head in disbelief. "This is Finland, dammit. Not North Haakovia or Iraq. I can't believe the Finnish government would—"

Katz held up his hand. "I don't think the government is behind it. I get the feeling we've got a rogue officer here, that Mallaskatu's been fighting this border war so long, against such a formidable enemy, that he's decided the rules of law no longer apply to him."

Manning twisted his wrists under the cuffs. "It won't matter who's behind it. Dead is dead."

McCarter spoke up. "I passed out again shortly after I came to," he said. "Then, when I woke up again, I heard them talking and pretended to still be unconscious. All I heard was one of the men say it would be Finland's word against North Haakovia, and who did they think the world would believe?"

James looked toward the back of the wagon. "Did you see the dude in the jeep carrying all the video equipment? My guess is they're gonna record the execution. Send Stensvik a home movie as a warning."

The truck halted, then moved on. Outside, the noises of the city faded, then disappeared altogether. Katz looked down at the stump of his amputated arm. The police who'd arrested him evidently *had* discovered the .22 Magnum hidden within the prosthesis. They hadn't returned the false limb as he'd hoped they might.

His last-ditch hideout weapon would do them no good.

With a quick glance toward the bars, Katz spit into his cupped hand. The tiny compass he'd pulled from his pocket and hidden under his tongue just before being searched popped out. He stared at it. They were traveling north-northwest.

Katz stuck the compass back in his mouth. North-northwest from Helsinki could mean they were headed anywhere.

Manning caught the Phoenix Force leader's eye. "You think if we—"

The loudspeaker came on again. "No speaking!" Mallaskatu thundered. "One more word and I will personally put a bullet in every man's head."

Manning turned away.

Katz took a deep breath. He had a plan. Not much of one, but the best he could come up with under the circumstances. And it certainly merited one last dangerous line. He turned to look down the line of warriors seated next to him. "Sixty twenty-seven," he whispered. "Twenty-two seventeen." He saw the puzzled looks on the faces of his men, but went on. "Here's the plan."

Immediately, before he could say another word, the wagon screeched to a halt. Mallaskatu jumped from the vehicle and disappeared from sight. A moment later, the rear door swung open.

Mallaskatu stuck the Valmet through the opening and jabbed the barrel inside. He frowned at Katz, then suddenly turned the weapon on the terrorist seated directly across from the Israeli. "Do you think I am playing games?" the colonel screamed, his eyes wild with hatred and power. "I am not!"

The colonel jerked the trigger and the terrorist's head exploded, spraying the concrete wall behind him with dark dripping tendrils of red.

Mallaskatu slammed the door of the wagon shut and returned to his seat. The vehicle started forward again. "If we must stop again," he said, pressing the microphone against his mouth, "I will kill you all."

CARL LYONS SAW the flatbed truck waiting at the end of the runway as Norton dropped the wheels of the Caribou onto the tarmac. The plane skidded to a halt, and Schwarz and Blancanales threw open the double cargo doors.

A dozen sailors in chambray shirts and blue dungarees hurried three large, and several smaller, crates from the truck to the plane.

Lyons lifted the mike. "Able One to Birdman."

"Come on in," Mott's voice came back.

"You got a fix on the Mallard's destination yet, Charlie?"

"Nothing positive," Mott replied. "But we're just west of Saint Croix in the Virgins right now. Hey...wait a minute." The radio clicked off, then came back on. "The duck's over Christiansted and dropping down. Repeat, descending over the island of Saint Croix. They must be planning to land somewhere near the east end, Able."

"Affirmative," Lyons said. "Keep them in sight. We're loading the counterterrorist package at Rosie Roades right now. Be airborne again shortly. Don't let them spot you if you can help it, Birdman." He keyed off.

Lyons turned in his seat and looked through the slats as the first of the big crates came on board. A flicker of a smile touched his lips as he saw what Kurtzman's magic computers had determined they might need.

The contents of the box made it look like Able Team had taken a few days off to vacation in the Caribbean. But what they were about to get into would be no vacation. You didn't take sarin, or soman, or whatever other types of biochemical weapons Stensvik had smuggled across the Atlantic, on a picnic.

The Able Team leader turned to Norton as the sailors continued handing equipment through the doors to Schwarz and Blancanales. The Delta Force pilot sat impatiently behind the controls, as anxious as Lyons to take off again.

"How we doing on fuel?" Lyons asked.

Norton glanced down to the gauge. "About half. You want to top it off now, while we're on the ground?"

"No time," Lyons replied. "We've got more than enough to make Saint Croix. If we don't stop now, we might get lucky and catch them on the ground."

The pilot snorted. His face took on a weary countenance. The man's body looked twenty, his face sixty, and Lyons guessed his age at halfway in between. But in the deep wrinkles weathered into the Delta soldier's skin, Lyons saw more experience than most men get in a century.

"Luck?" Norton said. The wrinkles deepened slightly, and he glanced over his shoulder toward Schwarz and Blancanales. "I don't know exactly who you guys are," he said. "Just that I've got orders to take *your* orders. But the three of you don't strike me as guys who count on luck."

"We don't," Lyons told him. "But we'll damn sure take any of it that comes our way."

"That's it!" one of the sailors shouted above the roar of the engines. Schwarz and Blancanales slammed the doors.

Lyons lifted the mike as the Caribou started down the runway. "Able One to Birdman," he said. "Where are you, Charlie?"

"Circling the east end of Saint Croix," Mott's voice came back. "The Mallard's landed near the shore. Stuff being unloaded...looks like they're getting ready to refuel. Yep, here comes the truck."

Lyons breathed a silent sigh of relief as the Caribou took off and started toward St. Croix, the Virgin Islands. The U.S. Virgin Islands. The Mallard was back in American territory, which would put Able Team back in their jurisdiction.

"Anybody else around, Birdman?" Lyons asked. "Civvies in the area?"

"That's a big affirmative, Able," Mott came back. "There's more tourists down there than you can shake a stick at."

Lyons's brief moment of optimism faded. "Roger, Birdman. Maintain surveillance. We're on our way." He started to hang up.

Mott's voice stopped him. "I can swoop down and get a pretty good angle on them with the .50, Able. I might be able to take them out without—"

"Negative! You read me, Birdman? Negative. Don't chance it, Charlie. You rupture any of those canisters and we'll have an island full of dead innocents." He paused, letting up on the mike with his thumb, then pressed it again. "Wait till we get there, Birdman. If we have to take them there, we'll have a better chance with two planes."

"You're the boss, Hoss. But like I said, they're re-fueling. They might take off again as soon as they've got go-juice, and I'm getting low myself. Don't know how far I'll be able to follow."

Lyons frowned. He glanced at the instrument panel. "We're nearing Fajardo. You got enough fuel to stay up until we get there?"

"Sure."

"Okay. You can touch down at Christiansted as soon as we get them in sight. We'll leapfrog you and take over."

Mott's mike clicked again, and Lyons heard a sigh on the other end. "Okay. But as long as they've still got the chemicals on board..." His voice trailed off, then came back. "I just don't know where this is all leading."

"I don't know, either," Lyons said. "But we will before long. One way or the other, Charlie, it won't be much longer now."

DOWNWARD THEY FELL, plunging into the bowels of the castle as they grappled amidst a hailstorm of dust and shattered stone, the terrorist's arms windmilling the air, his feet pedaling as if he rode an invisible bicycle.

The floors above the explosion continued to crumble as the middle of the castle fell in upon itself. An ancient oak beam struck Bolan across the back and hurled him into Selin. The Executioner reached out, grasping the man's throat with one hand and stabbing the Desert Eagle into the terrorist's belly. Before he could pull the trigger, a jagged stone crashed down on his wrist. The big .44 Magnum boomed, the shot going wide.

More ragged rock rained over the men's heads as they rebounded off a wall miraculously left standing. Selin screamed. Through the thick dust, Bolan saw that one of the falling boulders had sliced the terrorist's face, opening a gash from cheek to chin. White bone protruded briefly through the abrasion, then disappeared as the cavity filled with blood.

They fell on, passing what remained of another floor, sliding down another wall. Bolan's fatigue blouse caught momentarily on the sharp point of a ruptured beam, slowing their descent.

The Executioner glanced down. Through the haze he saw the joists that had once formed a doorway hurtling up to meet them. Crooking an arm, he released his grip on the terrorist and hooked the naked frame, the splintered wood biting into the flesh beneath his armpit.

Selin screamed again and plummeted on. A second later, the Executioner heard a thud.

The force of the fall swung Bolan down and under the doorway, then upward. He shoved the Desert Eagle into his waistband, reached up with the other hand and grabbed the joist. The vibrating wood creaked with his weight as he continued to swing, finally coming to a hanging halt like a bodybuilder about to perform a set of chin-ups. He hung for a moment, catching his breath, his lungs burning from the dust and oxygen deficit. His ears still rang from the blast, and when he shook his head tiny particles of stone rolled down his neck from his hair. His eyes felt as if he'd just been shot in the face with a sand blaster.

His vision still impaired, the Executioner looked down. Below, a cloud of dust concealed wherever Selin had landed. Bolan looked over his shoulder. The doorway from which he hung led to the hall, most of which appeared to be intact. He kicked his legs forward, swung up, then back, and dropped to his feet in the hallway.

Stepping back to the edge, the Executioner looked down as the dust cloud settled. Two floors below, the chapel floor remained undamaged. He breathed a silent sigh of relief. As he'd hoped, the explosion had traveled upward. The mourners, and anyone else who had been below the chapel, should have escaped the blast.

As the dust continued to clear, the Executioner wiped his eyes and a prostrate form came into focus. Sigrid Selin.

He lay spread-eagled on his back next to where Edvaard Varkaus's coffin had previously stood. The terrorist stared wildly up at the Executioner. He swallowed, coughed, and a tidal wave of crimson jetted out of his mouth.

The Executioner rubbed more grime from his eyes, and the dripping red protrusion on which Selin had fallen became clear. With the same mysterious irony of a tornado that lifted a cow, twirled it through the air, then sat it gently back down on the ground unharmed, one of the candle holders next to Varkaus's casket had remained upright though the explosion. It had entered Selin's back, exiting through the sternum.

Selin's voice was weak as he spoke, barely audible above the distant clamor. "Kill...me, please." The slick, wet candle holder that had pierced his chest bobbed with the effort.

"Kill...me..." the terrorist pleaded.

Bolan answered the request by drawing the Desert Eagle from his belt. Aiming down, he sent a 240-grain mercy round drilling through Selin's head.

The Executioner holstered his weapon. Dodging the debris, he turned from the crater above the chapel and made his way toward the staircase at the end of the hall. The aerial bombing to the north continued, growing ever closer as he headed down the steps.

A moment later he found himself on the ground floor. Two teams of Green Berets and several dozen castle guardsman had cordoned off the crowd near the castle's front entrance. As he'd ordered, the doors had been sealed.

Sergeant Orwig, Corporal Lelchuk and the little mortician who had helped plant the bomb stood against the wall. Lelchuk's wrist was cuffed to the terrified man. The other sergeant, Skinner, stood in front of the crowd, his hands out, palms down, speaking calmly to the terrified mourners who hadn't counted on the war starting when they came to pay their final respects to the late president of South Haakovia.

Bolan grabbed Skinner by the arm and led him out of earshot. "Get them downstairs," he said, glancing overhead. "If Stensvik's planes are coming, ground troops will be, too."

Skinner and several of the other soldiers began herding the crowd toward the staircase. Janyte Varkaus suddenly stepped from behind a quartet of Special Forces soldiers who had been guarding her.

Bolan felt a quick rush of desire wash through him as the woman's pale blue eyes met his. He pushed the emotion to the side. "Has there been any word from General Markus?"

Janyte nodded. "He radioed in earlier. Our fighter planes have taken off. They've engaged the North Haakovians ten miles south of the river."

Bolan nodded. It made sense. If something hadn't gotten in their way, the bombers would have been here by now. He took Janyte by the arm and turned toward the stairs.

She pulled away. "No. My place is here."

"Not right now, it isn't," Bolan replied. "We've got to get you to the tunnel. To the underground bunker."

Janyte's faded eyes flashed angrily. "My place is *here,*" she repeated, raising her voice slightly. "Markus has sent troops. They should arrive any—"

Her words were drowned out as another explosion rocked the front of the castle. But even as the Executioner was thrown back, he knew this one hadn't come from the air. Still holding Janyte's arm, the warrior felt his back strike the rock. He slid to the ground.

As the smoke cleared, Bolan saw the ten-foot crater where the castle's wide front doors had once stood. Through the opening, he saw three dozen men dressed in the brown woodland camouflage fatigues of the North Haakovian army. Blue-and-white hooped T-shirts were visible beneath their open collars, reminiscent of those once worn by all Soviet special forces.

One of the North Haakovian commando teams still held the RPG-7 antitank rocket launcher. He raised it again as the others broke for the hole.

The Executioner rolled on top of Janyte, drawing the Desert Eagle. He saw several Green Berets and castle guardsmen open fire, downing the first wave of the attack. Shielding the president with his body, Bolan joined in, the Desert Eagle booming as it sent 240-grain death into the N.H. soldiers. He let up on the trigger as Sergeant Orwig and six of his Green Berets crossed into his line of fire.

Bolan tightened his grip on Janyte. "Let's go!" he shouted above the noise.

"No! I cannot. I must lead my people—"

The gunfire drowned her out again.

As the attackers moved closer, steady streams of riflefire sailed into the castle, ricocheting off the stone walls. The mourners shrieked in terror. Then a round caught Orwig in the spine and the Green Beret sergeant jerked like a marionette with palsy before collapsing on the floor.

Bolan jumped to his feet, reached down and pulled the president to hers. The gunfire continued as the N.H. commandos advanced, their small-arms fire sounding like a musical background accompaniment to the heavier thuds of the distant aerial bombs.

Outside, the RPG erupted again. Bolan pushed Janyte toward the basement stairs as the rocket widened the opening in the stones and two dozen more N.H. men appeared from out of nowhere.

Without further ado, the Executioner lifted Janyte Varkaus into his arms.

"I must—" Janyte coughed. "—I must lead . . ."

"With all due respect, Madam President," the warrior said as he sprinted down the stairs toward he tunnel, "if we don't get you out of here, you won't be leading anything."

THE CORPSE across from Yakov Katzenelenbogen bounced lifelessly as the prison wagon pulled to a stop. Katz watched as Mallaskatu and the driver opened their doors and stepped out.

A moment later, he heard the key in the lock and the back door swung open. "Get out," the colonel growled.

The men of Phoenix Force stood, still cuffed and linked together at the wrists. Through the doorway, Katz could see that they were parked off the highway in front of a row of pine trees. The soldiers from the jeeps that had followed stood forming an arc around the rear of the van, their assault rifles pointed at the door.

An unarmed man in civvies stood just behind the soldiers. A handheld video recorder was mounted on his shoulder and trained in the same direction as the rifles.

Katz dropped to a sitting position on the back of the wagon, then scooted off and took a step away from the vehicle to give Encizo room to step down. Manning moved forward, and the Israeli took another step away from the wagon. His eyes darted left to right, up and down, scanning the terrain. As he had guessed, the pine trees he'd already seen were the edge of a forest. If his compass calculations and estimated road time had been correct, they were roughly ninety to a hundred miles west of Helsinki.

The vague odor of salt water drifted through the trees, which meant they were also close to the sea.

Katz continued to move away from the wagon as McCarter, then James dropped to the ground. The black Phoenix Force warrior was linked to a terrorist from the other side of the wagon, and one by one Vaino's men came through the door.

Encizo leaned closer to the Israeli. "Your plan..." he whispered. "What—"

The barrel of Mallaskatu's Valmet jabbed Encizo in the belly. But instead of the soft flesh the colonel had anticipated, the sights struck the Cuban's washboard abdominal muscles. The rifle stopped as if Mallaskatu had poked it into a concrete wall.

The colonel's eyes blazed with the madness of combat stress as he raised the Valmet to Encizo's throat. "You will not *talk!*"

Encizo glanced at Katz. The Phoenix Force leader could read the question in the brown eyes.

Now?

Slowly Katz shook his head. "Sixty twenty-seven," he said loud enough for everyone to hear. "Twenty-two seventeen. And all of you should go to church." The words brought the stock of Mallaskatu's assault rifle around in an arc to crash against his cheek.

The Israeli tasted iron as he dropped to his knees. When he opened his mouth to spit, a bloody white tooth bounced out onto the ground. "What you are doing violates Finnish law," he stated, looking up.

Mallaskatu threw back his head and laughed at the sky. "In times like this, *I* am the law."

One of the soldiers jumped up into the wagon, unlocked the dead terrorist and let the corpse fall to the floor. Dropping back to the ground, he slammed the door.

The police lieutenant who had driven the paddy wagon said something to Mallaskatu in Finnish, and the colonel snorted. The lieutenant spoke again, this time angrily, then made a washing motion with both hands, shook his head and headed back to the driver's seat.

Mallaskatu laughed, whispered something to his men, then turned to the prisoners. "You will follow Sergeant Hannu," he said, indicating one of the soldiers. "If even one of you speaks, all of you will be shot."

The sergeant started down a path into the trees. The terrorist on the other end of the chain fell resignedly in behind him. Katz brought up the rear as they moved into the forest.

The Israeli frowned as the line of men walked along the path like galley slaves on their way to the ship. His men probably wondered what the numbers meant, that was no problem. Katz had no doubt the men of Phoenix Force would figure that out for themselves given a moment to think. But if Encizo, or any of the others had not caught what the numbers were....

Katz glanced up at Mallaskatu, who was walking to the side of the line. He had heard the colonel's threat about one man talking and all of them dying before, in the van, when he had shot the man across from him. But the Israeli knew men like Mallaskatu too well. It wouldn't happen.

The crazed colonel wanted this done right. He wanted the video that showed the captured terrorists and Phoenix Force being led to the slaughter and executed. He wanted proof that would show Stensvik and Vaino that Finland would deal harshly and systematically with terrorism.

The falling footsteps within the peaceful Scandinavian forest frightened several sparrows in the trees. The birds flapped their wings, taking off against the bleached blue sky above.

No, Katz reasoned. At most Mallaskatu would shoot the one man who talked, and the chance was worth it. At this point Phoenix Force needed the numbers he had given them more than they needed him.

Katz took a deep breath as he saw Sergeant Hannu enter a clearing. "Sixty twenty-seven," he shouted at the top of his lungs. "Twenty-two seventeen and dammit, go to church!"

Mallaskatu's Valmet swung toward him, the hole in the end of the barrel looking wider than the gates of hell.

5

"I'm sorry Mr. Brognola," the secretary said. "But I've already told you the President is in conference with Prime Minister Nugent."

Seated behind his desk in the Justice Building, Hal Brognola fought the desire to rage. "And I told *you* this is an emergency," he said.

The secretary sounded confused, as if the burden of making decisions was too much. "He told me under no circumstances was he to be interrupted."

"Ms. Lightfoot, it's urgent that I—"

"I'm sorry, Mr. Brognola. But the President left his orders."

Brognola slammed the phone into the cradle, frustrated. Leaping to his feet, he peeled his jacket off the back of his chair and shrugged into it on his way to the door. "Kelly," he said as he stopped in the outer office for his briefcase, "have a driver downstairs by the time I get there."

"Do you want—"

Brognola was out the door and down the hall before the woman could finish her question. The elevator rose to meet him with maddening slowness. As soon as the doors opened, he stepped into the car and pushed the button for the ground floor. As the car started down, the big Fed opened the briefcase and removed the cellular phone. He tapped the number for Stony Man Farm into the instrument, and as soon as he heard Barbara Price's voice, said, "Give me an update on Able Team."

"They're nearing Saint Croix. The seaplane's on the ground refueling."

"Tell Lyons we've run into a snafu getting permission for an encounter outside U.S. territory," Brognola said. "I'm on my way to the White House now." The elevator door rolled back and he hurried through the lobby, the phone still pressed against his ear. "Tell Lyons to hold off as long as possible." He hung up.

Department of Justice Agent John Garrison jumped from behind the wheel of a government model sedan and opened the door as Brognola bounded down the steps in front of the building. "The White House, John. Fast."

A moment later they were sailing through the streets of Washington, lights flashing and siren blaring. Brognola tapped the buttons on the cellular phone again, calling the security office at the front gates of the White House and alerting them that he was on his way. "I don't want any delays," he growled.

The nervous voice of a uniformed Secret Service man assured him there would be none.

Brognola tapped the flash button and dialed the Oval Office direct. The first line he tried was busy, and he felt his diastolic pressure jump upward again.

Suzanne Lightfoot answered the second line on the third ring. "Please hold," she said without preliminaries.

Before he could object, Brognola heard a click and he was put on hold.

The Justice man was still on hold when Garrison slowed at the White House gates. The guards waved them through and Garrison pulled up to a side entrance. Brognola was out of the back seat before the vehicle quit rolling. He halted briefly at the door while a pair of Secret Service agents ran a handheld metal detector up and down his body before passing him through.

Brognola hung up, then dialed the Oval Office again as he stepped onto the elevator.

The secretary's voice spoke as the doors closed. "Yes, may I help you?"

"It's Brognola again. Is the Man still in his office?"

"Yes. But Mr. Brognola, *please*. You're first on the list as soon as the President and Mr. Nugent are finished—"

The elevator doors opened and Brognola stepped forward for another frisk by the Secret Service. "Don't bother," he said into the phone as he moved toward the door outside the Oval Office.

"Sir? Do you mean—"

Brognola opened the door and stepped inside the outer reception area. "I mean don't tell him to call me," he said into the phone. "I'm here."

The secretary looked up in confusion.

Brognola started toward the door to the Oval Office, where two more Secret Service agents stood guard.

"Sir!" Lightfoot said again.

The Secret Service men stepped in front of the door. "Mr. Brognola," a wiry-muscled man wearing a carefully trimmed mustache said tensely. "Sir, I know you outrank us at Justice, but we can't allow you to go in."

Brognola saw the confusion in the agent's eyes. He would have felt sorry for the spot in which he'd put the man if he'd had time for such thoughts.

Instead Brognola thought of Carl Lyons, Gadgets Schwarz and Rosario Blancanales. He pictured the plane that carried them, exploding, and bits and pieces of the fiery aircraft dropping into the sea.

The big Fed rammed the cellular phone up under the chin of the Secret Service man. The agent's head jerked back, then he closed his eyes and fell to the side.

The other agent, clean-shaved and broad-shouldered beneath a tapered blue suit, stared at Brognola, frozen. The Justice man took advantage of the momentary shock to drive a fist into the man's abdomen. The agent doubled over and Brognola shoved him out of his way. "What the hell," he muttered as he opened the door and stepped into the Oval Office. "They can only take your pension away from you once."

SOMEWHERE IN THE BACK of his mind, filed away and dormant since some junior high school geography class, Carl Lyons remembered memorizing the fact that the wooded hills on the island of Saint Croix rose over a thousand feet above sea level.

As he looked down now, he saw the stone buildings and pastel-colored houses of Christiansted flash by. To the south was a small mountain. Mount Eagle? The name seemed to ring a bell from the same mental file. Beyond the mountain, whatever its name, flat green plains rolled southward to the sea.

Lyons raised the microphone to his lips and said, "Pull off and refuel, Birdman. We're coming up on you now."

"Affirmative, Able," Mott replied. "I'm on my way."

The Caribou dropped closer to the ground as the east end of the island appeared. Lyons saw the landing strip below. Coupled to a refueling truck by a thick rubber hose, the Mallard seaplane was parked at the end of the runway. Three men stood by the tank, while another three had walked to the edge of the landing strip to ogle the bikinied women on the beach.

Lyons followed their line of sight. Less than a hundred yards from the runway he saw men, women and children in multicolored swimsuits moving about the picnic tables. More tourists stretched across the sand on towels and reclining chairs.

The Cessna's engines roared over the Caribou as Mott flashed by on his way to Christiansted. Lyons sat back, pondering the alternatives as Norton guided them past the beach and out over the water. He knew they wouldn't take the seaplane without a fight—the incident at Harmony Cove had proved that. But gunfire meant risking the rupture of the canisters containing the chemicals.

Lyons felt the muscles in his forearms tense. Okay, it was a risk. One hell of a risk. But what was the alternative? To let them go? Give them time to get the deadly biological agents positioned where their poison would do even *more* harm?

There was a third alternative—to try to take them in the air. Then, if the chemicals got loose, they had a chance of dissipating over the sea. *If* Able Team could time it so they weren't over land.

Lyons pulled a map of the Caribbean from his pocket and spread it on his lap. Puerto Rico, the Dominican Republic, Haiti and a dozen other populated islands met his eyes. He had no idea where the seaplane was headed, but wherever it went, there would be people.

Norton broke into Lyon's thoughts, summing up the Able Team leader's dilemma with a simple, "What now?"

"Circle over them one more time." Lyons keyed the radio mike. "Able One to Birdman." He waited for Mott's acknowledgment, then went on. "Charlie, how long had they been refueling when you left?"

"Not long. They'd just started."

"Able One out." Lyons stared down, watching the wake of a powerboat and water-skier near shore. The President's face suddenly flashed across his mind. At the moment they were in U.S. territory. But if the plane took off again...

"Able to Stony Man," he said into the mike.

Barbara Price responded immediately. She'd anticipated his question. "Negative, Able One," she said. "Still no word from the Man."

Lyons felt the queasiness in the pit of his stomach as he made his decision. He hated to go against the President. But if it came down to that and saving lives...

"What's the situation on the sub?" he asked Price.

"Delta's got it secured. One of the Haakovians on board sang like a bird. They were headed toward Havana."

Lyons dropped the mike to his lap. It made sense. Stensvik had Castro in on the deal. That meant the Mallard's final destination was more than likely Cuba, as well.

The Able Team leader sat silently for a moment. None of the options he had were good, and no amount of wishing was going to change that fact. It was time to make a decision and stand by it. He turned to Norton. "Buzz down where they can see you," he ordered. "We can't take them here, but at least we can keep them from taking off with full tanks."

"You got it." Norton swung the Caribou back around then dived suddenly, passing less than a hundred feet above the refueling seaplane.

The faces of the men on the ground jerked skyward.

Lyons stared down through the window as Norton rose in the air, then circled back again. The men outside the plane remained where they had been. "Give them a taste, Norton," he said. "Take out as many men as you can, but keep your fire away from the plane."

Norton nodded and the Caribou dropped through the sky again. The Delta pilot's thumb pressed the button, and a volley of gunfire stitched the tarmac to one side of the Mallard, huge ruts appearing in the tar. Norton twirled the gun and fired again. The three men on the runway fell under the assault.

Two of the men at the fuel tank ripped the hose from the plane, jumped into the truck and streaked away toward the terminal as the Caribou rose again. The third man disappeared into the Mallard.

A moment later, the seaplane taxied down the runway.

Norton took the Caribou down again, firing, hitting the tarmac on both sides of the Mallard and forming a tunnel of flying tar through which the seaplane passed. With Norton and Able Team on its tail, the Mallard rose into the air and headed west over the island.

"Drop back again," Lyons ordered as they passed over Christiansted. "Give them room. We'll follow them on radar."

"You're the boss." Norton cut the engines and the Caribou slowed, dropping back several miles until the tiny dot ahead disappeared in the sky. Lyons punched the Scan button on the programmable radio, and the red dot bopped across the screen, halting on a frequency each time it sensed a transmission. None of the transmissions sounded as if they came from the Mallard.

The Able Team leader wasn't surprised. If Castro had equipped the seaplane, and by now Lyons was certain he had, the man would have supplied it with a private frequency.

Lyons watched the beep on the radar screen as the Mallard continued to rise, finally leveling off and heading northwest. A few minutes later the shores of the Dominican Republic appeared. Five minutes after that, they were following the north coast of the island over Santiago. The radio began to buzz with local air officials demanding that both planes identify themselves.

Norton glanced over to the Able Team leader.

Lyons shook his head. He leaned over again, glancing at the control panel in front of the pilot. They'd used up a good deal of their fuel, and he wondered briefly if it had been a mistake not to refuel when they'd had their chance. "Hindsight," he muttered. "Twenty-twenty."

As they neared San Felipe de Puerto Plato on the north edge of the Dominican Republic, the dot on the radar screen suddenly dipped south, away from the sea. Norton followed it over La Vega, then San Juan before the seaplane began a zigzag course westward toward the coast.

Lyons no longer had any doubts. They were heading toward Cuba, all right, and the plan of the Mallard's pilot was to stay over populated areas where they couldn't be shot down without killing the people below.

Turning back north again at Govaives, the seaplane flew low over the fishing port of Anse Rouge, then Baie de Henne and Bombardopolis. Lyons pulled the map out again as they neared the village of Mole St. Nicoles on Haiti's northwest tip. Cuba lay just across the Windward Passage, less than fifty miles away.

Lyons turned to Norton. "Pull up on them," he ordered. "We've got to do something. There's no longer a choice."

Norton gunned the Caribou, and it shot forward in the sky.

But as it did, something that Carl Lyons had always known was proved to him once again. There was always a choice. No matter how late it seemed to be in the game, no matter how foregone a conclusion seemed to be, there could always be surprises.

As they pulled up on the seaplane, the Mallard suddenly jerked in the sky.

Lyons breathed a sigh of relief. His idea had panned out.

The Mallard was out of gas.

He watched the seaplane's pilot guide the craft to a landing on the blue waves halfway between Cuba and Haiti.

AUTOMATIC ROUNDS PEPPERED the stone walls above them as Bolan raced down the steps toward the tunnel with Janyte Varkaus cradled in his arms. The woman's perfume wafted up into his nostrils with every labored breath he took, reminding him that she wasn't only the president of a country about to be decimated by more civil war but a warm, beautiful and desirable woman, as well.

The Executioner pushed the thoughts from his mind. Right now, distractions like that were about as helpful as a pair of broken legs. He reached the basement floor and stopped, dropping Janyte to her feet and looking down the hall.

The Green Berets and castle guardsmen had herded the mourners and other civilians within the castle against the wall.

"We've got to get to the tunnel," he said. "You've got a country to run, and you can't do it from here. You've got a choice—I can carry you, or you can run with me."

Janyte looked at the civilians. "I can run. But what about them?"

"We'll have to hope the attack can be held off until Markus gets here," the Executioner said. "My first responsibility is to you."

A Green Beret suddenly appeared at his side carrying a handheld walkie-talkie. "General Markus *is* here, sir," he informed Bolan. "His troops are a block away now."

As if to emphasize his statement, the gunfire on the floor above suddenly intensified.

Bolan turned back to Janyte. "Let's go. There's still the chance some of the first strike could break through before this settles down. And if they do, you'll be their target."

Janyte nodded.

The warrior broke into a jog, holding the woman's arm. Janyte led him down the halls, through a confusing series of underground bends and turns, past emergency sleeping quarters and storage rooms. The gunfire faded as they ran.

Finally they reached a darkened side hall, and Bolan pulled a Mini-Mag flashlight from his pocket and twisted it on. Ahead, through the open archway, he saw a wing of the castle cellar that looked as if hadn't been used for centuries. Cobwebs as thick as cotton candy covered the stone walls, and the musky odor of decay filled the air. Rats scurried about their feet as they hurried toward a closed door.

A thick film of dust covered the rotting wooden surface. Bolan reached out and gripped the knob, which came off in his hand. He took a step back, kicked and the door splintered.

The Executioner stepped inside. More rats raced across his feet, frightened by the unaccustomed presence of humans. He raised the light and saw that the room had once been a wine cellar. Fragments of decayed wooden casks, scattered among the white bones of tiny animals, lay about the floor.

Janyte walked to the wall where a large boulder jutted from the other stones. She pushed gently, then harder. Turning to the Executioner, she said, "I need your help."

Bolan hurried to the stone and pushed. He heard a series of thuds within the wall, and slowly the stones parted, exposing a two-foot crack.

The warrior stepped through the opening and aimed the light down the narrow tunnel, where it tried to pierce a wall of dust as thick as fog. Less than six feet high, the tunnel opened to about three feet just inside the opening, then tapered sharply, leaving a passage barely wide enough for the Executioner to squeeze through.

Bolan twisted around and took Janyte by the hand. He nodded back toward the ancient wine cellar. "Is there a way to close it?"

She pointed toward another rock that jutted from the wall. Bolan pushed. This time, the thuds deep within the wall sounded quickly, and the stones moved back into place.

Bent almost double, the Executioner kept Janyte's hand in his as he led the way down the narrow tunnel. "How far is the bunker?"

The South Haakovian president coughed through the dust. "A mile. Perhaps a little more."

"Any other way in? Any place where Stensvik's men might cut us off?"

Janyte shook her head.

They took off again, covering a quarter mile before Janyte's raspy breathing forced Bolan to stop. He waited in the narrow confines, taking his own deep breath of the dusty, pungent air.

As soon as the woman had caught her breath, the warrior turned to her, noting again how her soft blue eyes contrasted so sharply with her coal-black hair. He started to speak, but Janyte beat him to it.

Smiling up at the Executioner, she said, "We are safe. Thank you."

Bolan opened his mouth, but before he could answer, the explosion behind them knocked him back against the wall.

As the smoke cleared, the first man dressed in the uniform of the North Haakovian army stepped through the debris and pointed his AK-74 down the tunnel.

YAKOV KATZENELENBOGEN stared into the hole in the end of the Valmet as Mallaskatu rested the barrel on the bridge of his nose. The colonel racked the bolt of the weapon, sending a sharp metallic click through the quiet forest.

The sun drifted down through the branches of the tree above him at just the right angle for Katz to see all the way down Valmet's sixteen-inch barrel. In the chamber he saw the sharp nose of the full-metal jacket 7.62 mm NATO round that was about to end his life.

The next thing the Phoenix Force leader knew, he was on the ground. But the pain he felt was in his chest, and he realized that Mallaskatu must have brought the stock up and into his sternum.

"Lift him up!" the colonel ordered.

Katz felt hands drag him to his feet.

"Do not speak again!"

The procession moved along the forest path. They entered the clearing, and through cloudy eyes Katz saw a wall constructed of weathered, unpainted lumber. The light gray wood was covered with reddish-black blotches at chest-level, and below the blotches, thin streaks ran all the way to the ground.

Katz's vision cleared further and he realized what the stains meant. They marked the places where bullets had passed through the men who had stood at the firing squad wall in the past.

"Line them up!" Mallaskatu ordered.

As a soldier led the chained men to the wall, the video camera began humming in the hands of the photographer.

Six Finnish soldiers armed with Sako TRG-21 bolt-action rifles took their places, twenty yards in front of the line of condemned men. Slowly and dramatically, aware that they, too, were being recorded, they loaded their weapons with one bullet.

The rest of the soldiers took positions on both sides of the wall. They dropped their automatic weapons to the ends of their slings, but kept their hands on the pistol grips, the barrels pointed loosely toward the chained men.

Mallaskatu motioned toward a corporal. The man pulled out a key and unlocked the chain from the terrorist at the end of the line. He moved swiftly along, yanking the links from the wrists of the rest of the men. The cuffs remained on.

The colonel stepped forward, taking a place between the shooters and condemned men. "You are terrorists," he said. "Cowards, scoundrels and murderers." His chest puffed out importantly. "But we are civilized men. Do any of you have final words? Would you like to take this time to repent for your lives of infamy? To tell of your regrets?"

A sniffle came from one of Vaino's men. Then the terrorist broke out in tears and fell to his knees sobbing. Two soldiers pulled him back to his feet.

Katz could think of a thousand words he'd like to voice—most formed questions. He had no intentions of killing the innocent Finnish soldiers who undoubtedly thought they were carrying out the lawful executions of war criminals. But was it right to spare the Finns if it meant that the men of Phoenix Force would die?

"Yes," Katz said. "I have words I would like to say."

All heads in the clearing turned his way.

"Then speak," Mallaskatu growled. He motioned the video camera to focus on Katz.

"My one regret," the Israeli said, "is that I grew up in a country where football was not played."

The clearing became silent. Mallaskatu's mouth fell open in astonishment. "What did you say?"

In the corner of his eye Katz could see that the expressions on the faces of the men of Phoenix Force were ones of concentration. They knew they were about to receive some kind of coded orders, and they were ready to sift through whatever subterfuge he threw out to fluster the Finns.

"Football," Katz repeated. He paused for breath, silently praying that the word "football" would mean the same to the Finns as it did to most people the world over. In most countries football meant what Americans called *soccer.*

And when Katz said what he was about to say next, he knew that small difference might be all that stood between life and death for the Stony Man warriors.

Mallaskatu's eyes narrowed, and Katz could see the colonel was trying to decide if his prisoner had lost his mind under the stress of imminent death. After a long moment the Finn's face softened, then took on the expression of a sadist pausing to humor his victim before the next round of torture. He motioned for the camera to keep rolling, then said, "Continue."

"There is one play that always fascinated me," Katz said. "So simple, yet often so effective. And sometimes the only way to save the game." He took a deep breath.

In the next few seconds the warriors of Phoenix Force would be free—or dead on the ground.

"The quarterback sneak," the Israeli said. He studied Mallaskatu's eyes, silently thanking God for what he saw there.

The Finnish colonel didn't have a clue as to what a quarterback sneak was.

But Calvin James knew. The black Phoenix Force warrior had played American football on the sandlots of Chicago, and was the first to react. Gary Manning, who had played the Canadian version, was right behind him. Charging suddenly forward, the two Phoenix Force warriors sprinted toward the firing squad.

Katz dived toward Mallaskatu as McCarter and Encizo raced for the other members of the firing squad. The terrorists against the wall took their cue from Phoenix Force, bolting toward their would-be killers with the vengeful screams of men taking their last slim chance.

For a split second the members of the firing squad froze. It took another second for them to raise their rifles, another to pull back the bolts.

Which was all Phoenix Force needed.

As the firing squad fumbled to slide their rifle bolts forward, a few short bursts of gunfire opened up from the soldiers at the sides of the wall. Katz saw two of Vaino's men go down, then the assault weakened as they neared the firing squad.

Manning and James reached the Finns and hit two men with tackles that would have bought them both tryouts with the San Francisco 49ers. Encizo and McCarter were less than a step behind.

Katz ducked his head, driving a shoulder into Mallaskatu's ribs as the colonel grappled for the pistol in his flap holster. The air shot from Mallaskatu's lips like a punctured balloon as the portly man hit the ground.

Afraid of hitting their fellow soldiers, the men positioned at the sides of the wall stopped firing suddenly, as Phoenix Force and the terrorists merged with the firing squad. Katz fell on top of Mallaskatu. Rising to his knees, he saw the rest of his team grappling with the soldiers. Then the autofire resumed as they began to break off and scatter for the trees.

The Israeli ripped the pistol from Mallaskatu's holster and pressed it under the man's chin. "Hold your fire!" he demanded of the Finns, and suddenly the clearing went silent.

Phoenix Force and the terrorists continued to disappear into the forest as Katz motioned for the colonel to get his feet. Using the startled man as a shield, he dragged him backward away from the wall.

The soldiers started to advance.

"Stay back!" Katz commanded, drilling the pistol barrel deeper into the soft flesh of Mallaskatu's neck.

The Finns halted in their tracks.

Katz dragged Mallaskatu on until he felt the bows of a pine on the other side of the clearing scrape his back. Pulling the colonel behind the tree, he swung the man around to face him.

Mallaskatu sneered. Saliva shot from his lips as he said, "You will never get—"

The colonel's own pistol ended his words as Katz brought it butt-first down over the man's head. He slumped to the ground.

Katz tapped his swollen eye as he spoke to the unconscious figure at his feet. "We're even," he said, then turned and sprinted into the forest.

6

"Well," Norton said as he guided the Caribou over the landing seaplane. "It's just like you said. We'll take any luck that comes our way."

Lyons nodded as he watched the waves through the windshield. Cuba lay less than thirty miles ahead. The fact that the Mallard had run out of fuel and been forced to land in the Windward Passage did seem like a stroke of luck. It now appeared that the only thing necessary would be to radio in for an American naval ship to come out and take over.

So Lyons did, relaying the message to Barbara Price who agreed to contact the Navy.

The Able Team leader sat back in his seat as Norton continued to circle. Yeah, he thought. They'd been lucky.

There was only one problem.

It hadn't been Carl Lyons's experience, either as a cop or as the leader of Able Team, that real life ever turned out quite that simple. Able Team in particular rarely drew their share of kings and aces, and he didn't see any good reason why the fates would choose this moment in time to change the way they dealt the cards to the team.

Blancanales cut into the ex-cop's thoughts. "Worked out pretty good. It doesn't look like the President was going to get back to us in time anyway."

Norton circled back over the plane. "What do you want me to do now?" he asked. "Head back?"

Lyons hesitated. Something was playing at the edges of his mind, and whatever that something was had caused his stomach to turn sour. "No," he finally said. "Just keep circling." He picked up the microphone. "Able One to Birdman," he said. "Where are you, Charlie?"

"In the air again and headed your way," Mott's voice came back. "I should be on top of you in a couple minutes."

"Roger. The Mallard's down."

"Huh?"

"Ran out of gas."

"So what do you want me to do?"

Lyons's uneasiness grew. "Come on in anyway. Better safe than sorry." He replaced the mike and stared down at the plane floating on the waters below.

Something was wrong. He could feel it—not just in his stomach now, but in the prickly sensation at the back of his neck that felt like someone had put too much starch in his shirt collar.

Lyons couldn't see a problem below. Or hear one or touch one or taste one.

But he could damn sure *feel* that something was wrong.

The decision didn't come from his brain. It came from the gut instincts that had kept the ex-cop alive on the toughest streets in America. "Gadgets, Pol, get the gear ready," he said suddenly. "We're jumping."

Norton's head jerked toward him as if pulled by a magnet. "You crazy? What for? There'll be a Navy gunboat here in a few more minutes. They can take care of this thing a hell of a lot better than three guys on water scooters."

Lyons ignored the question. "Take her up, Norton. Get us just high enough to jump."

The Delta pilot shrugged and pulled back on the controls. The Caribou's nose lifted as they sailed back over the seaplane again. Lyons, Schwarz and Blancanales broke open the equipment cartons and began slipping into scuba gear and parachutes. They double-checked the other crates, attached cargo chutes, then opened the double cargo doors and shoved them through.

The big boxes fell to the end of the static line, and the cargo chutes opened.

"Circle back one more time," Lyons ordered. "We'll go then."

Norton nodded. "You're the boss. But I still don't see why—"

A large blur suddenly appeared on the waves below. "Wait," Lyons said, reaching across the seat to grab Norton by the arm. "Drop down again. Let's see what we've got."

Norton pushed forward on the control and the Caribou dived lower. As they neared the blur, the obscure object came into focus. Lyons made out the distinctive lines of a Soviet Kirov-class battle cruiser.

A Cuban flag flew from a mast.

NO RISK, NO OBLIGATION TO BUY...NOW OR EVER!

GUARANTEED

PLAY "ROLL A DOUBLE" AND GET AS MANY AS FIVE FREE GIFTS!

HERE'S HOW TO PLAY:

1. Peel off label from front cover. Place it in space provided at right. With a coin, carefully scratch off the silver dice. This makes you eligible to receive as many as four free books and a surprise mystery gift, depending upon what is revealed beneath the scratch-off area.

2. Send back this card and you'll get hot-off-the-press Gold Eagle® books, never before published. These books have a total cover price of $15.49. But THEY ARE TOTALLY FREE; even the shipping will be at our expense!

3. There's no catch. You're under no obligation to buy anything. We charge nothing—ZERO—for your first shipment. And you don't have to make any minimum number of purchases—not even one!

4. The fact is thousands of readers enjoy receiving books by mail from the Gold Eagle Reader Service™. They like the convenience of home delivery... they like getting the best new novels before they're available in bookstores... and they love our discount prices!

5. We hope that after receiving your free books you'll want to remain a subscriber. But the choice is yours—to continue or cancel, any time at all! So why not take us up on our invitation, with no risk of any kind. You'll be glad you did!

THE GOLD EAGLE READER SERVICE™: HERE'S HOW IT WORKS

Accepting free books puts you under no obligation to buy anything. You may keep the books and gift and return the shipping statement marked ''cancel.'' If you do not cancel, about a month later we will send you four additional novels, and bill you just $13.80*—that's a saving of over 10% off the cover price of all four books! And there's no extra charge for shipping! You may cancel at any time, but if you choose to continue, then every other month we'll send you four more books, which you may either purchase at the discount price . . . or return at our expense and cancel your subscription.

As he watched, two smaller monohull crafts suddenly shot away from the warship and skirted across the water toward the seaplane.

"Oh-oh," Schwarz said.

The prickly feeling at the back of Lyons's neck disappeared and was replaced with the adrenaline surge of upcoming battle. He had no doubt what the two speedboats carried.

Cuban frogmen. Ready to unload the chemicals and get them first to battle cruiser, then into Havana before the U.S. ship arrived.

Lyons hurried toward the open cargo doors. He followed Schwarz and Blancanales out of the Caribou into the air. He had time for one brief thought before he pulled his rip cord.

Able Team was well out of their jurisdiction, and the President still hadn't gotten back to them.

"Sorry, sir," Lyons said into the wind as his chute opened. "I know you're a busy man. But we've waited about as long as we can."

STILL A MILE from the Caribou, Charlie Mott breathed a sigh of relief. He didn't mind battle—that's what he'd been trained for, and besides flying planes, about the only thing he'd ever been very good at. But considering the possible consequences of rupturing even one of the canisters, it was far better that the seaplane was about to be taken peacefully.

Mott flew over the Mallard and began to circle back. The Caribou passed overhead as he reached for the mike. He glanced into the side mirror and blinked several times.

Damn, he could use some sleep. He was beginning to see things. If he hadn't known better, he'd have sworn he just saw parachute canopies.

Mott keyed the mike. "Birdman to Able, come in Ironman."

A voice he didn't recognize answered his call. "Able are on their way down right now, Birdman."

Mott blinked again. He *had* seen chutes. But what could have caused Lyons to change his mind so quickly that the Able Team leader hadn't even informed him?

Mott turned again, back toward Cuba. He dropped lower, and saw first the tiny dots streaking toward the seaplane, then the slower Soviet-made warship. He wondered briefly what he might be able to do from the air to help Lyons, Schwarz and Blancanales. But the question was short-lived. Charlie Mott knew the answer.

Nothing. Like always, the men of Able Team were on their own.

AUTOMATIC RIFLE FIRE ricocheted off the stone walls, sailing by like a flock of angry hawks as the Executioner pushed Janyte Varkaus ahead of him down the tunnel. The South Haakovian president slipped and fell, and another burst of 7.62 mm rounds flew above their heads. Without breaking stride, Bolan reached down, caught her arm and hauled her back to her feet. Lifting her into the air, he raced on, away from the pursuing N.H. soldiers.

The Executioner's mind raced as fast as his legs as he made a sharp turn in the tunnel. The ancient people who had dug the route had known what they were doing. Well aware that an escape might include pursuit, they had included twists and turns that would enable them to have at least occasional cover.

The problem was, it had been flying arrows they'd had in mind, not bullets.

Bolan dragged Janyte down the tunnel. The South Haakovian president tripped suddenly, falling forward onto her hands and knees and scooting across the sharp stone. The Executioner reached down as he ran, scooping her back to her feet and taking her hand. He felt the warm, sticky blood from her scraped palm on his. Glancing down, he saw the skinned knees beneath Janyte's shredded nylon stockings.

As they neared the next turn, the men behind them rounded the last corner. More bullets flew past them down the narrow tunnel, the roars threatening to deafen them in the confined space. Bolan pushed Janyte around the corner, then stopped. He peered back, extending the Desert Eagle and squeezing the trigger.

The soldier leading the pack fell in his tracks. A man behind him tripped over the body, somersaulting across the rock. Bolan leveled the big .44 and put a round between his eyes as he came out of the roll. The third man in the procession vaulted the two bodies. He zigzagged forward, several frag grenades bouncing on the assault suspenders on his chest.

Bolan fired, missed, then fired again. Behind the leader, he saw at least a dozen more soldiers. A gunner cut loose suddenly with a burst that drove the warrior back around the corner. Grabbing Janyte's arm, he turned and sprinted on.

The Executioner reached down, patting his belt. He had one magazine left for the Desert Eagle. Two extras for the Beretta. Not nearly enough to hole up and make a stand.

But he had to do *something*. They were still at least a half mile from the compound, and sooner or later one of the bullets would hit home.

They came to the next turn a moment later. Bolan ducked around the edge and halted again. "Go on," he told Janyte.

The woman looked up at him wearily. "I can't," she choked.

"Yes, you can! I've got to slow them down somehow. Now go!"

With a look of concern Janyte limped away.

Bolan heard boots pounding along the tunnel and peered back around the corner. The man wearing the assault suspenders had outdistanced his comrades by a good thirty yards. He slowed to a jog as he cautiously neared the turn.

The warrior waited until he reached the wall, then stepped around the corner and fired point-blank into the man's face. As the soldier slithered to the ground, the Executioner's arm reached toward the grenades on his chest.

A blanket of riflefire forced him back around the wall before he could reach the explosive devices. Four more men, each gripping a short-barreled carbine of some sort, sprinted toward him.

The Executioner fired two more rounds down the tunnel, slowing the men, then looked down at the body in front of him.

The man in the suspenders lay on his back, less than three feet away. The grenades were fully exposed on his chest, but there was no way the Executioner could reach them without putting himself at great risk.

Bolan aimed the Desert Eagle at the man on the ground and took a deep breath. Slowly, aiming more like an Olympic Slow-Fire pistol contestant than a combat soldier, he steadied the sights on the pin of the nearest grenade. Letting out half his air, he squeezed the trigger.

The Desert Eagle roared. The pin in the end of the grenade disintegrated and the handle flew back.

The Executioner was on his feet and running, mentally counting off the seconds as he raced down the hall. If the North Haakovians hadn't seen what he'd done, there was a good chance they'd be on top of the grenade when it exploded. Even if they were aware of the grenade, they'd be forced to retreat momentarily.

The exploding grenade would ignite the others on the suspender belt. With a little luck, the tunnel would be blocked.

The force of the explosion threw the Executioner onto his face. Debris and dust pelted his body, and when he finally hauled himself to his feet, his ears roared like a freight train had driven through his head. He paused, waiting for the ringing in his ears to subside.

Behind him, just around the corner, he heard the sounds of men digging through the debris.

Bolan turned and sprinted on. Okay. The plan had worked.

Just not quite as well as he'd hoped it might.

He caught up to Janyte just after the next turn. The South Haakovian president sat against the wall on the floor, her chest heaving.

The warrior helped her up. "I've slowed them down," he said as they moved on. "But they're still coming." As if to emphasize his words, the pounding of combat boots against the stone floor behind them echoed down the tunnel once more.

Janyte's breath came in high-pitched gasps as they rounded the final turn. A wide steel door stood fifty yards directly ahead. Gun ports had been cut into the stone walls on each side, and the barrels of rifles extended through the holes.

The woman tripped again, rolling across the floor. The Executioner lifted her into his arms and staggered toward the door, offering a silent prayer to the universe that the men behind the gun ports would recognize him, his uniform or their president. It would be an ironic end to be blown away by friendly fire after all they'd just been through.

The prayer was answered. The rifle barrels drew back into the compound. The steel door swung open, and Bolan saw a man wearing a South Haakovian major's uniform standing in the doorway. Two more officers stepped to his side, urging on the Executioner with words of encouragement.

The sound of boots pounding the rock filled his ears again as the pursuing N.H. troops rounded the final turn. The carbines opened up, the rounds skidding off the stone walls to slam against the wall at the end of the tunnel.

Bolan was less than fifty feet from the door when the sudden impact hit him between the shoulder blades. He felt his arms go limp as the force threw him forward onto his face. Janyte skidded from his paralyzed arms as he slid through the open door into the compound.

Vaguely, as if from another world, Bolan heard the door slam shut behind him. Then the dull sounds of the rifles firing through the portholes met his ears.

The ambiguous knowledge that people were squatting next to him sank into the Executioner's brain. He heard soft, feminine crying, and through blurry eyes saw a woman wearing a torn black dress. Her hose hung in tatters from her calves and thighs. Blood covered her hands and legs.

Bolan felt a soft hand on his face. "Don't die," the woman sobbed. "Oh, God, please don't let him die."

Bolan wondered briefly who she was. Then his mind raced back over the years, quick twinklings of gunfights with mafiosi, Communists, drug dealers and terrorists flashing before his eyes. He saw his mother, father, sister and brother, and for a brief instant, the Executioner smiled.

He had fought the good fight. He had done what he could to make the world a better place, safe from human predators who preyed on the weak and innocent.

And this was as good a way as any to die.

As the woman sobbed on, the Executioner closed his eyes.

CALVIN JAMES DREW BACK a fist and propelled it into the face of the man in the Finnish sergeant's uniform. The Sako bolt-action rifle dropped from the man's hands.

James looked quickly around amid the confusion and saw the other members of Phoenix Force pummeling the men of the firing squad. The paradox they were in struck the Phoenix Force warrior.

Each punch diminished the threat from the men with the Sakos. But each punch increased the probability that the soldiers with automatic weapons at the sides of the wall would begin firing again as their comrades hit the ground and were no longer in the line of fire.

James saw Manning bring a huge hammer fist down on the skull of a Finnish corporal. The man hit the dirt like a peg being driven into the ground.

A short burst of fire sailed Manning's way.

"Scatter!" Katz shouted at the top of his lungs.

James took the order willingly as he felt the heat of several 9 mm rounds fly by. Some days discretion really was the better part of valor, and as far as the ex-Navy SEAL was concerned, today was one of those days.

He turned and sprinted toward the trees.

More rounds blew his way. James saw the movement as they struck the leaves ahead and sent bark flying from the trunks of the towering pines. Grass and dirt flew between his feet as a burst slapped the ground a foot to his left. He dived forward, going into a shoulder roll ten feet from the tree line.

When he popped back to his feet, James found himself just inside the low branches of a pine tree. He dropped to all fours, crawling under the limbs, the tree's sharp needles digging into his back. As soon as he was under the branches he rose to his feet and sprinted deeper into the forest.

Two numbers pounded in his head in time to his labored breathing as James dodged the sturdy trunks like a tailback racing toward the end zone.

Sixty twenty-seven. Twenty-two seventeen. Go to church.

What in the hell had Katz meant?

The former Chicago street kid was a half mile from the clearing when he finally allowed himself to stop and turn back, scanning the trees for any sign of pursuit. He cleared his mind and tuned his ears, listening for cracking twigs, the fluttering wings of frightened birds, or the quick movement of a startled rabbit. His nostrils flared in the chilly Scandinavian air as he strained for a scent of the enemy drifting through the trees.

Nothing.

James turned and walked, deeper into the forest. He didn't know what the numbers meant, but right now he had more immediate concerns. The Finnish soldiers might not have started after him yet, but as soon as they had regrouped, they would. And they would do so with a vengeance, having been humiliated by the escape.

He needed a weapon.

James's gaze dropped to the ground as he walked on. He had little hope of finding a hard rock in the forest. The tall pines meant deep roots, and deep roots meant the earth beneath was soft. Perhaps a spear could be made from one of the drier branches....

An opening suddenly appeared through the branches and James smiled. A natural clearing, a place where the trees wouldn't grow. He jogged toward it.

He stopped at the edge of the trees and dropped to his knees, his fingers digging into the soil. Ten inches down, he struck shale. He rose to his feet and ventured farther into the clearing, his eyes scanning the ground until they fell on a slab of the hard rock roughly fifteen inches long.

"Forget the knife. How about a short sword?"

James lifted the slab and slapped it against the ground to dislodge a family of insects that had set up housekeeping on the bottom surface. Ten feet away, he found a rounded chunk of cobblestone and he grinned. He had his hammer stone. Now all he needed was an anvil.

The former SEAL found it in the middle of the clearing, a relatively flat piece of shale even larger than the one he planned to use as a knife blank. Dragging it quickly out of sight inside the trees, he knelt and went to work.

James pulled his shirt over his head and used it to pad the anvil. He placed the knife blank strategically on the other stone and held it with his left hand, studying the strengths and weaknesses of the grain. Then, raising the hammer stone high above his head, he brought it down against the shale.

The slab split in halves, exposing two flat cores.

Skillfully James worked the hammer stone around the edge of one of the pieces with quick, even strokes. He frowned when he'd finished, noting the thick edge midway up the blade. It was in a difficult position, and direct percussion wouldn't take care of it.

The Phoenix Force warrior searched quickly through the chunks of shale he'd chipped from the sides until he found a suitable "punch." Then, using his forearm to secure the blank, he chipped away until the edge was uniform from spear point to handle.

He sharpened the edge against the hammer stone, then held his finished product to the sun for examination. It might not compete with the best that Al Mar, Cold Steel or SOG Specialty Knives had to offer, but it would have to do in a pinch.

The pinch came quickly.

James heard the rustle of dead pine needles behind him and rolled behind the nearest tree. He rose to a squatting position, the shale blade held in a hatchet grip, hidden behind his thigh.

With the hatchet grip, he had four working surfaces available at a moment's notice. The edges or point could kill a man instantly if the noise turned out to be one of Dag Vaino's escaping terrorists. But he would use the blunt pommel end if the approaching sound turned out to be one of the soldiers.

The footsteps drew nearer. James heard the man move toward the clearing, just to his left. He waited.

A moment later, a face peered uncertainly from behind a tree six feet away. Sweat covered the tightly drawn features, and the man's shirt had been torn.

James recognized the face. It was the same terrorist who had dropped to his knees and cried like a baby seconds before Phoenix Force had led the escape.

Yes. Phoenix Force had helped Dag Vaino's terrorists escape.

James didn't like the way that sounded.

Slowly, silently, the ex-SEAL moved from behind the tree trunk, duck-walking through the branches toward the pine where Vaino's man stood peering into the clearing. The stone dagger hidden behind his back, James rose to a crouch.

He was less than four feet away when his foot crunched a dried twig hidden beneath the needles that carpeted the ground.

The terrorist turned his way, and raised a heavy branch high above his head. Then he stopped.

The fear left the terrorist's eyes. He dropped the club to his side, his lips forming a smile of relief as he saw that James wasn't one of the soldiers, but a fellow prisoner.

James didn't like that very much, either.

So he smiled back. Then, with a lightning-fast movement he had learned on the streets of Chicago, James brought the shale blade from behind his back and stabbed the rock-knife deep within the terrorist's chest.

Bracing his left hand on the man's shoulder, he drew the knife out and ran the edge across the man's throat. The terrorist fell to his death before the smile could leave his face.

James wiped the weapon across the man's pant leg and started across the clearing.

Now. If he could just figure out what the hell sixty twenty-seven twenty-two seventeen, and the deal about the church meant.

THE WAY GARY MANNING saw it, he had two immediate objectives. He had to figure out what orders Katz had tried to give with his weird numbers and statement about going to church. The Phoenix Force leader had risked his life twice to make sure the men of Phoenix Force heard the two clues, so they had to be important. But first, Manning had to find a way to stay alive long enough to figure it out.

Manning's heavy leather combat boots pounded the earth faster than he ever remembered his Nike running shoes doing when he trained on the back-country roads outside Montreal. Of course he had a stronger motivation for this run than he did when he was just trying to stay in shape.

The bullets flying after him did a damn good job of urging him on.

The big Canadian risked a quick glance over his shoulder as he neared the edge of the trees. The soldiers near the wall had already started after their escaping prisoners. And two of them had chosen him as their prey, angling off toward where he was about to duck into the woods.

Manning's hand fell unconsciously to his side where the Beretta 92-S should have been. His fingers fell on the empty holster. He raised the hand as he entered the tree line, mopping sweat from his eyebrows with the back of his sleeve.

His shoulder brushed past a long-dead tree branch as he dodged around the trunk. The dried wood snapped like a matchstick, flying in front of his face. He reached up, catching it and frowning down at the rough bark.

The demolition expert dropped it and ran on. Too thin. And too brittle for what he had in mind.

Behind him, Manning heard voices as his pursuers entered the woods. Their boot steps didn't slow, and why should they?

They didn't have to worry about him stopping and setting up an ambush. They had disarmed him themselves.

Manning spied a break in the trees and angled toward it. He found himself suddenly on a narrow hunting path and quickened his pace. The path brought a quick round of memories of the countless hours he had spent hunting big game in the Canadian wilderness. He was grateful for that time, for the sport of the hunt, but more particularly right now for the experience it had given him in the woods.

That experience might mean the difference between life and death.

The boots behind him became louder. Manning raced on, the knowledge that the men behind him were gaining ground not lost on him. He was being forced to go too fast to cover his tracks, but the Finns were following too quickly to be noticing snapped twigs and footprints anyway.

That meant they knew these woods like the backs of their hands. They had known he would run into the hunting trail, and they knew he was still on it.

Yeah, he knew woods all right. The problem was, he didn't know *these* woods.

A high-pitched voice shouted behind him, and Manning heard an explosion. The bullet whizzed past his head and into the trees, shaving pine needles from a branch like a machete. The Phoenix Force warrior hooked a bend in the path and moved out of sight.

Okay. The Finnish soldiers knew what he was going to do even before he did it. That meant that sooner or later they'd catch up to him. Sooner, if they knew a shortcut that intersected with the hunting path.

Manning saw another break in the trees. He left the path, twisting and turning past the pines like the rugby fullback he had once been at McGill University. A favorite maxim of his old coach crossed his mind: the best defense is a good offense.

Manning was often surprised at the thoughts that popped into his head under stress. At first many of them seemed unrelated to the predicament in which he found himself. But over the years, he had learned better than to dismiss them outright without first considering what subconscious message they might be trying to convey. A few times, those messages had crystallized into coherent thought.

And saved his ass.

The big Canadian slowed as he neared the clearing: the best defense is a good offense. Suddenly the thought didn't seem so strange, and it became perfectly clear what he had to do.

Something totally unpredictable.

He stopped at the edge of the trees, his eyes searching the ground. He spotted a dead branch roughly the circumference of his arm and lifted it in both hands.

The branch was shorter than he'd have liked, maybe a foot and a half long. But he had no time to look for the perfect club. He wasn't likely to find a Louisville Slugger lying around the forests of Finland.

Pivoting, Manning sprinted back toward the trail. The boot steps of his pursuers grew louder. He recalled his old coach again, words the man had spoken just before the University of Toronto match his senior year, when McGill had been the two-to-one underdog.

We have surprise on our side.

Manning would be relying on surprise again. And again, he was the two-to-one underdog. Worse if you considered the rifles in the hands of the opposing team.

As he hit the hunting path again, memory of the fact that McGill had lost the match years ago crossed his mind. But as he brought the heavy pine limb down over the head of the first surprised Finnish soldier, Manning realized that it hardly mattered.

He would win today. Because he would not accept defeat.

Manning drew the club over his head again as the second startled Finn froze in his tracks. The branch crashed down into the man's face sending a geyser of blood spurting from his nose, a scream from his lips.

The Phoenix Force warrior stood above the fallen men, looking down. He dropped the stub of wood and knelt next to the first soldier, drawing the pistol from the man's flap holster and thumbing off the safety. Quickly he rifled the men's web gear, appropriating another pistol, both Valmets and extra magazines for the guns.

In the breast pocket of the first Finn, Manning found a compass. A tubular map case hung from a sling over the second man's shoulder. The Canadian ripped it away and added it to his growing equipment supply.

Manning checked the men's pulses once more, then rose to his feet and jogged down the hunting trail. He felt the comforting bumps of the assault rifles against his sides.

The big Canadian stopped suddenly in his tracks, his hand falling over the smooth leather of the map case. A grin started at the corners of his lips, spread upward, and then he found himself laughing out loud in the quiet woods.

He had accomplished the first of his two objectives—he had stayed alive long enough to figure out what Katz's crazy numbers had meant.

And without knowing it, Manning realized as he stroked the smooth leather, he had accomplished his second objective at the same time.

RAFAEL ENCIZO KNEW he'd been lucky. First, he'd escaped the clearing without getting shot. Then, the soldiers seemed to have overlooked him when they chose their paths of pursuit.

But he knew that meant two things: that luck could change at any time, and that the Finns who had missed him when he scampered into the woods would be chasing the other members of Phoenix Force.

Encizo intended to make sure that neither he nor the rest of the team got caught.

The Cuban hurried through the trees, stooping occasionally to bend under branches of the abounding pines. He paused every few yards, his ears reassuring him that there were still no sounds of pursuit in his direction while his eyes scanned the area for the items he knew he needed. Coming to the site of a campfire—at least three days old—he saw several partially burned sticks amid the coals.

He knelt and sifted through the ashes, finding three long, straight sticks that had been intended for kindling but had been too green to burn. He slapped them against his knee. Not ideal, but sturdy enough. And the best he was likely to find under the conditions.

Moving on, Encizo scanned the branches he passed. He came to one roughly six feet long and an inch and a half in diameter. He grasped it in both hands and jumped into the air, throwing his body weight down.

The branch bent, but didn't break.

Encizo dropped back to the ground and unclasped his belt. He used the serrated edge on the front of the buckle as a saw blade, scoring a neat line around the limb. He quickly cut down into the branch, then upward. This time, the limb snapped down into his hands.

The Cuban worked quickly, clearing the branch of twigs and needles. He frowned when he saw several knots along the shaft, then went on. He wasn't in a sporting-goods store. He couldn't expect the long bow to come flawlessly out of a box wrapped in packing paper.

A cold breeze drifted through the Scandinavian forest as Encizo finished clearing the limb and then planed it with the SwissChamp's knife blade. Jabbing the end into the ground, he knelt on one knee and placed his left hand in the center. His right went to the top of the stave, and he pulled lightly toward him. The bow turned in his left hand and settled into its natural bend.

Encizo sharpened the ends of the three sticks he'd found, then reached into the pouch again and removed a coil of heavy fishing line. He notched the tips of the branch with the SwissChamp's small pen blade, attached the line and took off again through the trees.

The Cuban frowned as he jogged over the soft carpet of pine needles covering the forest floor. He knew the limitations of the weapon he'd just constructed.

For one thing the arrows had no feathers—they wouldn't fly true over a few feet. Well, he'd work within his limitations, as he always did.

Fifteen minutes later, the Cuban heard footsteps. He slowed to a walk, creeping over the needles with the same dexterity his Indian ancestors had centuries before. Voices sounded ahead. He dropped to all fours, taking up a position behind a tree trunk and peering through a break in the branches.

A moment later, three Finnish soldiers appeared on a narrow path in the trees.

A thin smile broke out on the Cuban's square face. The men were being careless, assuming their prey was unarmed. That would work to his advantage.

Encizo nocked an arrow and waited as the soldiers drew closer. Then more footsteps drifted through the trees on the other side of the path, and the Finns dropped back out of sight into the pines.

David McCarter stepped tentatively out of the trees and scanned up and down the path.

A moment later, three rifle barrels jabbed into his neck and sides.

McCarter raised his hands.

Encizo drew a deep breath as the Finns stepped onto the path. He waited as they whispered something at the Briton, then one of the men dropped his rifle slightly.

The Cuban felt the muscles in his forearm tensing, frantic to draw back the arrow and let it fly. But he knew he had to wait until at least one more of the men relaxed, dropped the barrel of his Valmet away from McCarter. If not, they'd fill the man full of holes before his primitive bow could take them out.

As the soldiers continued to talk, a tall man with sandy blond hair falling below his camouflage DI cap reached into his pocket and pulled out a pack of cigarettes. He stuck one in his mouth, and when he did the Valmet fell to the end of its sling.

Encizo didn't hesitate. Aiming toward the soldier who still covered McCarter, he closed one eye, drew back the arrow and released it. The quickly constructed weapon twanged loudly as the arrow spiraled through the air, sinking into the Finn's upper thigh.

The man looked down in surprise.

Encizo already had the second arrow in place when McCarter drove an elbow into the soldier's face, knocking him to the ground. The cigarette fell from the blond soldier's mouth as he turned in Encizo's direction. The Cuban sent another shaft flying through the opening in the pines. It struck the soldier in the elbow, skimming off the skin but causing the man to grab the joint with his other hand and yelp in shock.

McCarter finished the job with a quick front snap kick to the testicles. The Finn dropped to his back, clutching his groin. The yelps continued, but they now came from pain rather than astonishment.

Encizo had pulled back the last arrow when the third soldier suddenly circled an arm around McCarter's neck and shoved the Valmet under his chin. "Halt! Do not move!" he yelled into the forest in accented English. "Or I will kill your..." He paused, searching for a word. "Colleague," he finally said.

The Cuban's hand froze, the arrow pulled back and resting against his cheek.

"Come out of the forest!" the soldier demanded. "Now! Or I will kill him!"

Encizo started to rise. Then suddenly, he heard a stirring in the pines behind McCarter and his captor. He saw a blur of movement above the Finn's shoulder, then something descended onto the soldier's head with a dull thunk. The Finn's eyes closed, and the rifle fell from his hands as he slumped to the ground at McCarter's feet.

Encizo watched as a man stepped out onto the path, a pistol dangling from his lone arm.

The Cuban rose to his feet and moved through the trees.

Yakov Katzenelenbogen smiled wearily as Encizo stepped onto the path. The Israeli's eyes fell to the homemade bow in his comrade's hands, then dropped to the Valmets on the ground next to the three unconscious Finns.

"Grab a rifle," the former Mossad agent said. "Or maybe you'd rather just keep the bow."

Encizo chuckled as he and McCarter retrieved the Valmets. "No, I was almost out of arrows anyway."

Katz led the men into the trees, saying, "Do you remember the numbers I gave you?"

"Yeah," the little Cuban replied. "I remember. But I haven't had a whole lot of time to figure them out yet."

"Well, I could explain it, I suppose." Katz grinned over his shoulder as the men of Phoenix Force broke into a trot. "But it would be so much more fun just to show you."

7

Lyons watched the Cuban speedboats race toward the Mallard as he fell through the air. He squinted, trying to block out the bright Caribbean sun obscuring the plane.

Was it his imagination, or was the Mallard riding lower in the water than it had before?

Below, Schwarz and Blancanales had already hit the water and released their chutes. The thin nylon blew across the waves in the wind, then slowed as it became saturated and finally sank out of sight.

The big ex-cop shoved the regulator to his air tank into his mouth a second before his feet hit the water. He squeezed his nose through the face mask as he descended, clearing his ears. His other hand tapped a button on his console unit and sent air shooting into his buoyancy vest.

The Able Team leader stopped abruptly, twenty feet below the surface. Another tap of the button propelled him up again. He turned a full one-eighty as his head broke back into the air, and he floated atop the waves of the Windward Passage.

Fifty feet away, he saw Gadgets and Pol snapping the metal bands on the insulated crates with pry bars. He hurried through the water toward them.

The crates had been broken open by the time he reached his teammates, and three shiny black Jet Skis floated in the water.

Lyons pulled himself up onto the nearest water vehicle as Schwarz and Blancanales mounted the other two. With three sudden roars and a flash of water behind them, Able Team started toward the Mallard.

Across the waves, on the other side of the seaplane, the Cuban boats raced toward the same objective.

Lyons twisted the throttle, urging more speed out of the Jet Ski. He stared at the plane. No, it wasn't his imagination. The plane was sinking. Some type of damage must have occurred when they ran out of gas and were forced to land unexpectedly on the rough water.

Automatic gunfire broke out from the other side of the plane, but the Cuban's rounds fell short. Able Team raced on, zigzagging through the water when they finally were in range.

Lyons heard a sudden grunt. Whipping his head to the side, he saw Pol fly from his Jet Ski as if a locomotive had driven into his chest. "Go on!" the Able Team leader shouted at Schwarz. "Get set up!" He let up on the throttle and turned back.

Blancanales floated faceup in the water when Lyons reached him. The Able Team warrior's eyes were clamped shut.

They opened as the ex-cop slowed.

"Damn!" Pol said as he climbed up in back of Lyons. His voice was weak. He coughed. "Ballistic nylon vests may stop bullets. But don't let anybody tell you it doesn't still hurt like hell."

A second later they were racing toward the seaplane. Lyons drew the Colt Python as they neared. Ahead, he saw Schwarz pull his Jet Ski to a halt in a blur of flashing water next to the Mallard's pontoons. The electronics expert grabbed an insulated floatation box from the back of the ski and dropped into the water.

Part of the equipment Kurtzman's computers had determined they might need had been a large supply of specially packaged phosphorous grenades. Enclosed in miniature buoyancy units similar to those that kept Able Team themselves from sinking through the water, the grenades were equipped with a primary explosive that would scatter secondary incendiaries through the water in a circular pattern.

Schwarz began distributing them around the downed aircraft. Once set up, they could be detonated either singly, in clusters, or as a whole with his electronic remote control.

The thunder of engines blasted overhead, drawing Lyons's attention. He saw both Mott and Norton circling the seaplane. He could almost feel the frustration he knew both men would be feeling, being so close to the action yet unable to help.

But the big ex-cop had no time to worry about Mott and Norton as his Jet Ski raced toward the Mallard. He had another battle approaching, a battle that might well be his last if he didn't focus every ounce of concentration he could muster.

And hope that, this time, a hell of a lot of luck really did find its way to Able Team.

Still under fire from the Cubans, Lyons cut a serpentine pattern closer to the plane. He focused on the

Mallard's cockpit as a gunner stuck a pistol through one of the windows, pointing the weapon at Schwarz.

Lyons dropped the Python's sights on the window and pulled the trigger. The enemy gun dropped into the water, the hand drew back into the plane.

The water was dangerously near the bottom of the Mallard's windows now, and Lyons knew that as soon as the cabin filled, the rate of the plane's descent would increase dramatically. He glanced back at the approaching Cuban boats and made out the lines of men dressed in scuba gear similar to his own.

He'd been right. The monohulls carried an army of Cuban frogmen. If the plane sank before Able Team could stop it, and the froggies were able to take out Schwarz, Blancanales and himself, they stood a good chance of retrieving the chemicals before the U.S. gunship arrived.

Thirty feet from the seaplane, Lyons let up on the throttle. The Jet Ski bounced across the surface of the water, its own wake moving up to push it on.

A bearded man wearing khaki pants and canvas deck shoes suddenly popped through the Mallard's window onto the wing. Lyons triggered the Python twice, catching the man in the neck and side. He slid off the plane to float facedown in the water.

The gunfire continued as the Cubans neared the plane on the other side. Lyons and Blancanales dived from the Jet Ski, thrusting their air regulators into their mouths.

As the Able Team leader dropped beneath the surface, he saw the first of the two Cuban boats slow on the other side of the plane.

THE EXECUTIONER'S first sensory response when he came to was the blast of gunfire. His second was the dull ache in his head. He moved slowly, finally getting himself up into a sitting position on the floor. The gunfire continued. His hand fell automatically to the holster on his belt, as he turned toward the noise. Then part of his memory returned and he realized he couldn't have been out more than a few seconds.

The soldiers firing through the gun ports suddenly stopped. "That's the last of them," one of the men said. He propped his rifle against the wall. "Sergeant Gundersson, send a mop-up party into the tunnel to make sure."

The rest of his memory—the attack on the castle, the air strikes, his escape through the tunnel, and then the final bullet that had downed him—came flooding back into the Executioner's consciousness. He let the hands of several uniformed men help him to his feet, then steady him as his head continued to clear.

A high-pitched voice sounded somewhere on the other side of the crowd. "Let me through! Let me through!" A man wearing a white lab coat and a woman in white nurse's dress pushed the soldiers away. The doctor wore round gold spectacles. He stopped in front of Bolan, then grabbed the Executioner's arm and led him through a door and down a hall. The nurse followed.

Bolan soon found himself facedown on an examining table. As the doctor ripped what remained of his blood-soaked uniform blouse away, he sensed Janyte again at his side.

The South Haakovian president reached down and took his hand.

The doctor prodded his back with some kind of cold instrument, and a moment later said, "Ah, here's the little culprit." He moved around the table into the Executioner's vision.

Bolan looked up. Gripped between the thumb and forefinger of the man's red-soaked surgical glove, he saw a .44 Magnum bullet.

The doctor squinted down at his bloody fingers. "You were wearing a vest?"

Bolan nodded. "It's rated for .44 Magnum, but that's fired out of a pistol. The longer barrel of the carbine should have built up enough velocity to penetrate the material."

The doctor frowned and leaned over him, inspecting Bolan's back again. The medic was shaking his head when he straightened. "You are a very lucky man, Colonel Pollock. You were evidently leaning forward when the bullet struck."

Bolan shrugged. "You don't lean away from the direction you're running."

The doctor nodded. "The bullet snagged momentarily in the nylon, which caused the vest to bunch and double. The bullet made it only halfway through, breaking the skin but doing no permanent harm." He removed his spectacles, pulled a handkerchief from his lab coat and began cleaning them. "After a few days you will be able to return—"

"I don't have a few days," Bolan interrupted. "Dress the wound, then I'm gone."

"Colonel Pollock," Janyte said, gripping his hand tighter. "Please . . ."

The doctor shook his head again. "I cannot allow it," he said. "I will place you under observation."

Bolan struggled to a sitting position on the table. "No you won't. Now either dress the wound, or get out of my way and I'll do it myself. There's a war going on upstairs, and I've got work to do."

"You soldiers are crazy," the doctor said. He blew air between his lips, then turned to the nurse. "Get my sutures and the gauze," he said resignedly.

"TURKU" MEANS TRADING post.

Situated on both banks of the Aura river, the city of Turku was founded early in the thirteenth century and served as Finland's capital until 1812. By the 1980s, the harbor village had grown to a population of 165,000 and was the country's third-largest metropolitan community.

Turku is known for the immense shipyards that spread along the Baltic Coast, its Finnish and Swedish universities, and the mild winters that allow the port to remain open when the harbors of most other seaside Scandinavian cities are frozen in.

These facts, while interesting enough to the men of Phoenix Force, were hardly vital.

What *was* important to Katz, Encizo, McCarter, Manning and James was Turku's location.

Latitude 60.27. Longitude 22.17.

Yakov Katzenelenbogen mounted the ancient stone steps of the seven-hundred-year-old cathedral, his gaze traveling up the face of the building. Helsinki might have stripped the seat of government from Turku in the early nineteenth century, but somewhere above the ground floor, the cathedral was still the seat of the Archbishop of Finland.

He entered the cathedral and moved quickly along the ornately decorated halls, mixing with tourists who gripped brochures of the site in their hands. He stopped outside the sanctuary to adjust his trousers; rough woolen pants that he had snatched from a clothesline just outside of town. They were far too large and itched, but they created the illusion he wanted to create—a poor Finnish country bumpkin who had come to visit the cathedral.

Katz opened the door to the sanctuary and stepped inside. Several heads were bowed in prayer in front of the pews. But none belonged to James or Manning. He walked slowly down the aisle, a quick wave of concern rushing through his chest. Had his coded orders been too vague? Had James and Manning been unable to figure them out?

Or was the situation worse than that? Had the Canadian and former Navy SEAL been gunned down in the forest?

Katz took a pew near the front. Then he leaned forward and closed his eyes. A second later, he felt a hand on his shoulder.

"Are you troubled, my son?"

Katz looked up to see Gary Manning's smirking face. The big Canadian wore a black sport coat and slacks, and the collar of a priest.

The Israeli couldn't suppress a smile. "Yes, Father. I have recently lost some very close friends."

"Come with me," Manning said. "Who knows? Perhaps they can be found. The Lord works in mysterious ways."

"Does he ever," Katz murmured as he rose from the pew. He followed Manning out of the sanctuary and down the steps of the cathedral where Calvin James stood wearing a black robe.

Katz stopped in front of James, his eyes traveling back and forth between the two men. "I guess when I told you guys to go to church, you took me seriously."

James chuckled. "We bumped into each other a few miles outside of town, near a little country chapel. These threads seemed less conspicuous than what we were wearing." He paused. "Don't worry. We left enough money in one of the offering plates to replace these things several times over."

Katz nodded. "I met up with David and Rafael. They're waiting down the block. Let's go."

The three Phoenix Force warriors took off down the street, stopping at a sleepy little coffee shop on the corner. A tall slender man stood at the window, painting the day's special on the glass. Katz opened the door and ushered the other two men inside.

McCarter and Encizo sat at a back table, watching the door. Their faces remained expressionless as their teammates crossed the room, but Katz could see the relief in their eyes. He took a seat across from McCarter and glanced up at the television set mounted on the wall across the room, distracted momentarily by the canned laughter from a Finnish sitcom.

"The first thing we need is wheels," he said.

"That's a big affirmative." James nodded. "Something that won't draw attention but's still big enough to hold us all."

The waitress appeared with coffee mugs and poured. She stared openly at Katz, then turned quickly away.

"Under the circumstances," he whispered as the woman walked away, "I'm not sure we can be too choosy." His eyes followed the waitress behind the counter. "How are we fixed for weapons?"

"James and I stashed what we took in the forest," Manning replied. "But we're low on ammo."

"Same with us," Katz said. "Which means we've got to rearm, as well." He glanced at the window facing the street as a late-model black Nissan Maxima pulled to a stop in the parking lot across the street. A portly man wearing a camel-hair overcoat exited the vehicle, stopped at the booth by the street and was handed a ticket through the building's tiny window. He crossed the street, entered the coffee shop and took a booth by the window.

The Phoenix Force leader turned back to his men as the fat man opened a menu.

"Okay," McCarter said. "We grab a car and guns. But then what? We've hit a dead end as far as Vaino goes."

Katz nodded. "Right. But I've got an idea." He rose from the table and crossed the room to a pay phone. Dropping a coin in the slot he tapped in the number that would eventually connect him to Stony Man Farm, then a credit-card number that if ever traced, would lead to a dummy corporation known as Bakersfield Industries.

Barbara Price picked up the receiver on the first ring.

"I need to talk to Kurtzman," Katz said without preamble.

As soon as the computer whiz was on the phone, he continued. "We've hit a brick wall, Aaron. See if you can tap into the CIA files, or Interpol or something. Somebody might have a new lead on Vaino's operation.''

"Oh, well. I guess this means I'll have to drop out of the kick-boxing championship I was supposed to fight in tonight.''

Katz chuckled. "I'll get back to you.'' He hung up and he was halfway back to the table when he saw the faces of his men suddenly harden.

Spinning on his heel, the Israeli looked up at the television and saw himself and the other members of Phoenix Force staring into the camera. The picture was obviously a frame from the videotape Mallaskatu had been shooting. Touched up to keep from showing that they were about to be illegally executed, it displayed the men from Stony Man Farm and Vaino's terrorists only from the waist up.

Behind the men, Katz saw the bloodstains on the wall in the forest clearing.

The waitress let out a gasp, then covered her mouth. Changing gears quickly, she turned to the grill behind her and pretended not to have noticed.

Katz nodded to his men and they stood. The Israeli walked calmly to the booth next to the window where the man in the camel-hair coat had just dipped a fork into his meal. He leaned down on the table and smiled. "English?'' he asked.

The man looked up in irritation, then nodded.

"I need the keys to your car.''

The fat man frowned.

Katz opened his tattered coat, exposing the grips of Mallaskatu's pistol. "I need them *now*.''

The fat man's mouth dropped open.

Katz circled his fingers around the pistol as the rest of Phoenix Force joined him.

The fat man reached into the side pocket of his coat and pulled out the keys.

"And the parking ticket," Katz added.

The man placed a stiff piece of cardboard on the table next to the keys.

Katz scooped up the ticket and key ring, and led his team to the door. In the reflection of the window, he saw the waitress hurrying toward the pay phone.

The warriors walked casually across the street to the parking-lot booth. Katz handed the ticket through the window along with a Finnish markma bill, then joined the others at the Maxima. McCarter slid behind the wheel, and Katz handed him the keys. A moment later they hit the street.

The men of Phoenix Force were two blocks from the coffee shop when the first police car arrived.

THE BATTLE HAD LULLED somewhat when the Executioner's helicopter touched down on the front line. The North Haakovian army, having at first pushed its way five miles across the river into South Haakovian territory, had been chased back by the arrival of U.S. troops secretly waiting aboard ships in the Gulf of Finland.

The Americans had come complete with the technological superiority that had crushed Saddam Hussein. That, and the heroic spirit demonstrated by South Haakovian troops intent on preserving their hard-won freedom from communism, had not only stopped the ground attack but had ended the aerial assault as well.

At least temporarily.

Stensvik's commando attack on Castle Larsborg had appeared to be successful at first. But the arrival of General Markus's troops had been the beginning of the end for the advance party of N.H. special forces. Those who hadn't fallen to fire in the first few minutes had been hunted down one by one in the streets of the capital.

But the destruction on both battlegrounds had been extensive. Several oil fields near the river still burned, their fires raising the temperature by ten degrees for miles around the river.

The reconstruction of the castle was already under way, but it would be some time before parts of the building would again function. The chapel, and everything between it and the roof, had been devastated by the bomb. That included the presidential suite on the fifth floor, and temporary quarters for Janyte Varkaus had been set up on the ground level.

Bolan ducked under the blades and jogged past an OD tent that stood on the edge of the forest. According to the topographical map, as well as several S.H. officers expert on the local terrain, the forest contained a series of widemouthed caves. Those caves would play a vital part in the Executioner's backup plan should things get hot again on the border.

The warrior passed the tent and headed toward the LAV-25 wheeled light-armored vehicle parked in the middle of a row of M-1 Abrams. As he ran, a series of shots rang out across the river, but for the most part the battle had ended.

The temporary calm didn't fool the Executioner. The war was hardly over. Stensvik was simply regrouping. And as soon as the North Haakovian dictator had time to catch his breath, the fight would be on again.

Bolan put a boot on a rear tire and boosted himself onto the vehicle. He had radioed ahead from the underground bunker, ordering that the commanding officers assemble for an emergency briefing. He had also ordered that a temporary mobile command post be set up by the time he arrived. He had chosen the LAV for several reasons. First was its speed. The Executioner knew that with the Russian technology available to Stensvik, it wouldn't take long for the North Haakovians to triangulate the radio transmissions of the S.H. forces. When that happened, the headquarters could be determined. Stensvik's bombers would return.

And that *would* happen eventually.

But there were other important considerations to choosing the LAV. The troop carrier was large enough to carry a small attack squad of crack U.S. Special Forces soldiers. The GM diesel engine and eight-wheel drive could propel the vehicle along the road at 60 miles per hour. It could head cross-country at between 17 and 22, all the while firing both a Hughes 25 mm Bushmaster gun and a 7.62 mm coaxial MG. The state-of-the-art armored car also boasted smoke-grenade launchers and a 360-degree view within the closed hatch of the gunner and commander stations, as well as run-flat tire liners and ballistic armor that withstood almost anything thrown at it.

Static scratched from the radio as Bolan took a seat inside. An American Marine who looked like he was into bodybuilding grabbed the mike from the console and handed it to the Executioner. "It's got to be for you, sir," he said, shaking his head. "General Markus has been trying to reach you every thirty seconds for the last half hour."

Bolan grabbed the mike as the general's voice came over the airwaves. "Base command to Colonel Pollock. Come in, Colonel Pollock!"

The warrior keyed the mike. "Pollock here."

"Do nothing until I arrive," the general ordered. "I will take command as soon as—"

Bolan keyed the mike again, cutting him off. "You can forget that, General. Stay put and look after the home place. I'm in command on the front."

More static popped across the waves as the general paused. Then the voice came back, angry. "What are you talking about?"

"Call your president. She'll tell you. Now, get off the radio before our buddies from the north figure out where we are."

The radio went dead.

A head popped down through the hatch. Bolan looked up to see the upside-down face of a freckled American soldier. "Sir, the officers have assembled as ordered."

Bolan nodded and pulled himself back up through the opening. He dropped down to the ground and headed to the tent.

Inside, the Executioner saw the rigid expressions on the faces of the commanding officers of both the Americans and their South Haakovian counterparts. The men who led the various battalions and specialized units scattered up and down the Inge river knew the significance of the battle they were about to resume.

If the N.H. army crossed the river again, troop moral would be nonexistent. From the river on into Larsborg would become a cakewalk for Stensvik's forces.

Bolan watched each man salute, then said, "I'll dispense with formalities. We don't have time." He lifted a wooden pointer and tapped his palm. "As you're all aware, we have an AWACS on its way. When it gets here, we can plan our counterattack as well as get a little advance warning as to when the enemy plans to strike again. Until then, we'll have to rely on the radar back in Larsborg."

A South Haakovian colonel with a thin pencil mustache cleared his throat. "Begging the colonel's pardon," he said in heavily accented English. "But won't our radio transmissions tip off—"

"They will, but it can't be helped. We've got to communicate. That's why we're running a mobile base." He tapped the map mounted next to him with the pointer and squinted toward the man's name tag. "Colonel Kuusamo, your men are planted here, in and around the border village of Kongsberg, right?"

Kuusamo nodded.

"Has the village been evacuated?"

"Yes. Those that were still alive are being shuttled into the capital right now."

"Good," Bolan said. "Keep your men there. Have them dig in with both feet. The river's shallow at that point, and we don't need any N.H. sneaking across."

The Executioner turned to a U.S. Marine major as Kuusamo left the tent. The man wore tree-bark cammies and looked like he might have been in every battle the Marines had undertaken since San Juan Hill.

Knife and shrapnel scars covered his face and hands. More scars cut into the dozens of tattoos that ran up and down his arms. "Major Brown," Bolan said. "I understand you've got a Battalion Recon Company as well as some Force Recons under your command?"

Brown's milk-white crew cut bobbed up and down. "That's affirmative, sir."

"Then get them across the river into enemy territory and do what you guys do best. I'll leave it up to you to pick your points of entry and specific missions."

Brown grinned. "How deep you want to penetrate?"

Bolan gave the man a hard stare. "All the way into Stensvik's bedroom if you get the chance."

"We will, sir. We'll *make* the chance." He saluted, then pivoted and marched out.

The Executioner went on down the line of commanding officers, tapping the map with his pointer and giving out orders until the last man had left to return to his troops. Dropping the wooden stick onto a desk, he opened the tent flap and started back toward the LAV.

For now, he waited. But as soon as the AWACS arrived, he would launch an all-out effort that would send Stensvik's men streaking back to Sturegorsk with their tails between their legs. And when they did, the Executioner would be hot on their heels.

Communism had all but died in Europe. Stensvik was the last holdout, and the Executioner had orders to kill him, and put an end to everything for which his insanity stood.

As he climbed to the top of the LAV once more, Bolan heard the sudden roar of engines. He looked up to see a squad of Russian Tupolev "Blackjack" bombers streaking across the sky from the north.

Franzen Stensvik might die, all right. But he didn't intend to go down without a fight.

AARON KURTZMAN STARED at the computer screen, his eyes glassy from fatigue.

"Damn. The spooks must have hired someone new to set up their programs."

Kurtzman sat back in his wheelchair and ran a hand through his hair. Someone had installed a new set of traps in the CIA computer intelligence files, traps that he'd immediately recognized, but had so far been unable to circle. Knowing that Phoenix Force needed a new trail immediately, he had broken out to check the easier-accessed files for Interpol, Britain's MI6, and German, Russian and Japanese intelligence.

No one had anything on Dag Vaino that he didn't already know.

Stony Man's computer wizard lifted the empty pipe from the stand and stuck the stem between his lips. The flavor of long-burned Cavendish rolled over his tongue, and he suddenly realized he hadn't left his console for nearly twenty-four hours. With that knowledge came the awareness that he was hungry, and that his bladder was desperate for relief.

On the other hand, Katz and his team needed to know where Dag Vaino was hanging out even more desperately.

Kurtzman leaned forward again, tapping a new strategy into the computer.

ACCESS DENIED. IDENTIFY IMMEDIATELY flashed onto the screen. He cut away from the linkup before his origin could be traced.

But each time he tried, the CIA's machines would pick up a little more, and Kurtzman knew he had only a few more chances before the Agency computer would realize that some unauthorized agency was trying to break into their files. That didn't bother him. The Farm couldn't be traced. He had set up the program himself, in a way that only a few men, in fact, only one man in the entire world besides himself could possibly—

Streck. The name popped suddenly into Kurtzman's mind. Danny Streck.

The computer man's fingers flew across the keys again, tapping numbers and buttons to form codes that would access the CIA's personnel files. They would be top secret, too, but he had cracked them last week and unless that code had been changed too...

It hadn't. Kurtzman breathed a sigh of relief when the words FINAL IDENTIFICATION appeared on the screen. He typed in the code name "Hiram," then the code number for the director of the U.S. Central Intelligence Agency.

Kurtzman grinned as he wiped more sweat from his brows. The director always seemed to get the least resistance. Besides, if you were going to do something, why not be the very best?

An alphabetical list of files appeared on the screen. Kurtzman hit the "search" button, entered the name, "Streck, Daniel P.," tapped the button again and sat back.

The computer clicked and gurgled. Two seconds later, a CIA employment dossier appeared. Streck's name was printed at the top. Kurtzman scanned the document. Danny Streck had been hired just three weeks before. He was the new supervisor in charge of the entire fleet of CIA magical mystery machines.

Three weeks. Plenty of time to set up the traps and new codes Kurtzman had been unable to work through all morning.

He shook his head, angry with himself. He should have guessed before this that the spooks had hired Streck. No one else knew the computer business like Aaron Kurtzman.

But Streck came close. At least close enough to waste several hours of the Bear's time.

The computer wizard's hands stopped above the keyboard as a sudden thought struck him. Now that he knew who was behind the new CIA program, he could eventually break it. Every computer man had certain predisposed prejudices and preferences. He had trained with Danny Streck, and knew the man's inclinations well. It was just a matter of time.

But time was something that was at a premium right now for Stony Man Farm. And he and Streck had not only gone to college together years ago, they had been roommates during several advanced training classes over the years. The quickest way to gain access would be to call up Streck and level with him.

Almost as quickly as the idea had struck him, it vanished. No, Streck was a professional. He wouldn't give out that information, regardless of how strong their friendship might be.

Kurtzman sighed. He started typing again.

8

Lyons leaped from the Jet Ski as the first of the two Cuban speedboats slowed on the other side of the seaplane. A dozen Cuban frogmen in black rubber dry suits squatted around the rails, each holding a flashing steel diver's knife or spear gun.

The Able Team leader heard Blancanales's splash behind him as he drew his own knife from the rubber sheath on his calf and dropped through the water beside the sinking plane. He tapped the inflator button and shot air into his vest, then swam forward, Pol at his side.

Lyons willed a mental message toward Schwarz, hidden somewhere inside the plane itself, urging him to push the button, detonate the grenades. He swam beneath the plane's belly, wondering what the hell Gadgets was waiting on. He saw several dark forms dropping down through the water on the other side. Okay, he and Pol would have to take out as many of the Cubans as they could with their blades. They were outnumbered six to one. For now. In the next few seconds, the second Cuban boat would arrive and those odds would double. But if they could slow things down at least, maybe the Navy would arrive to take control of the chemicals.

The water on the other side of the seaplane exploded suddenly. White foamy froth blew Lyons and Blancanales back from beneath the plane, flipping them through the water like gymnasts practicing backward somersaults. The Able Team leader breathed deep into his regulator, drawing in air more to fight the shock than for oxygen debit.

Lyons came to a stop and got his bearings. As the water cleared, he looked toward the surface. Six black-clad bodies floated on their bellies, flames and smoke rising through the air from the burning rubber.

Gadgets had waited until just the right time, waited so the grenades would do the most damage. And he'd eliminated half of the threat with the tap of a button.

The big ex-cop sheathed his knife, reached behind him and unzipped the main pocket of his backpack. He withdrew a bulky square of folded plastic. Blancanales moved in at his side, grabbed a corner and they spread it out.

Lyons shot back to the surface. He wrapped the Velcro strap attached to his end of the inflatable raft around the window post.

As he secured the Velcro, Lyons looked past the bodies to see the second Cuban speedboat nearing. It held as many men as the first.

Odds? Still at least six to one. Maybe as high as nine to one.

Submerging again, he saw Blancanales fastening the other strap to the tail of the plane. He reached into his pack and pulled out an adapter, holding his breath while he screwed it onto his regulator.

A flash of silver metal streaked up past his nose. Lyons's eyes followed it instinctively as the sharp metal rod sailed on out of the water to glisten in the sun.

He looked down, and saw directly beneath him a rubber-clad form flipping upward, clutching a ScubaPro diver's knife.

Still holding his breath, Lyons jackknifed in the water, drawing his own knife from its calf sheath. He flipped down to meet the oncoming frogman, darting to the side at the last second. His lungs screaming for air, Lyons swung the knife in an arc. He felt the tip penetrate the rubber, then the soft belly flesh beneath. The Able Team leader twisted the grip, and an explosion of bubbles shot from the Cuban's mouthpiece.

Lyons moved in closer, withdrawing the knife and ripping the Cuban's regulator from his mouth. He pressed it to his lips, drew in two precious lifesaving lungfuls, then sliced the hose.

More bubbles glutted the water around him as the Cuban's tank emptied. Lyons grabbed the man by the hair and spun him around until the buoyancy unit on his back was exposed. He plunged the tip of the knife into the air-filled backpack, then released his grip.

The Cuban frogman dropped to the bottom.

Seven down. Seventeen to go?

Lyons moved back to the raft and twisted the adapter onto the inflation stem. The raft began to inflate as he bled his tank of air. He didn't know how much air he'd have left when the floatation raft was full. Maybe none.

To his side, Lyons saw two more Cubans with knives flipping toward Blancanales. His heart told him to shove the regulator back in his mouth and rush to the aid of his teammate. His brain said no.

The first priority was to secure the plane, keep it from sinking. And if he, or Blancanales, or Schwarz, or all three had to lose their lives in the process, then so be it.

It went with the territory.

Lyons watched Blancanales draw his blade across the throat of one of the Cubans, and above him he heard the roar of the engine as the second speedboat arrived. The plane jerked as the hull bumped a wing, and the adapter was torn free from the stem.

The sudden jar was all it took to drop a window below the surface. Water shot into the cabin, and suddenly the seaplane was submerging.

Schwarz came swimming out of the window.

Lyons bled his vest of air and flipped after the plane, Schwarz at his heels. The Able Team leader heard a flurry in the water behind him and looked over his shoulder.

Schwarz and a frogman held each other in a death grip, both men trying to free their knife hands and plunge a blade into his opponent.

Lyons felt as if a tank rested on his chest as he caught up to the plane and grabbed for the stem. Pressure built in his ears. His thumb and index finger flew to his nose, closing off his nostrils beneath the mask as he desperately tried to equalize. He glanced to his depth gauge. Sixty-five feet. Not deep, but he had submerged far too quickly. He had crossed two atmospheres, and was in danger of—

A sharp pain shot through his side, and the Able Team leader twisted away from it. He felt something wet running down his ribs beneath his dry suit, and turned back to see a knife blade slashing through the water toward his throat.

The big ex-cop's hand shot up, catching the man's wrist. He dropped the adapter and brought his own knife up under the Cuban's chin, the point punching through the man's Adam's apple.

Lyons dropped the man and turned back to the seaplane.

It floated weightlessly in the water, seventy feet beneath the surface.

The Able team leader ripped the adapter from his air hose and shoved the regulator into his mouth. His vision blurred as the lifesaving oxygen filled his chest. He looked up. Gadgets and the Cuban were nowhere to be seen, but he could see the bottom of the second speedboat. Soft plops echoed down toward him as more men in black rubber dropped over the side.

Lyons's fingers encircled his knife in an ice-pick grip as he started up to meet the enemy. Suddenly another explosion of white light rippled the water and sent the Able Team leader head over feet. Pain filled his brain. He closed his eyes, wondering how close to the blast he had been. Then the feeling returned to his body and he tapped air into his buoyancy unit, floating and breathing easily as he waited for the water to clear.

A soft fizzle drifted through the water. Lyons breathed in, and the rubber around the metal regulator stuck to his mouth. He looked at his air gauge— empty.

Lyons held his breath again as he unfastened the weight belt around his waist. Slowly he began to drift upward. He slipped out of the buoyancy vest, opened the stem cover and took a deep breath from the air inside the unit.

As he rose, the water settled down and he saw more flaming, floating bodies. His head broke the surface in time to see Blancanales stick his blade into the last Cuban frogman.

A second later, Schwarz's head popped up next to him. Gadgets still held the remote-control detonator in his hand. All three of the warriors now turned their eyes skyward. Norton's Caribou flew over, dipping a wing, as did Charlie Mott's Cessna.

Lyons caught his breath, then looked out across the waves to the north. He could just see the large bulky shadow as it appeared on the horizon. He and the other two men of Able Team watched as the shadow neared.

A U.S. Navy warship.

Ten minutes later, Able Team was on board. Lyons's rib wound had been shallow, and the ship's doctor had disinfected it, then bandaged the man's chest.

The captain led them from the infirmary to the radio room, where the radioman ripped the headset from his ears and handed it to Lyons. "Somebody trying to reach you," he said.

The big ex-cop wrapped the receiver around his ears. He listened, said, "Roger," then took off the headphones and turned to Blancanales and Schwarz.

"Hal just heard from the Man," the Able Team leader said. "He gave us the go-ahead."

Blancanales and Schwarz broke up.

CALVIN JAMES SAT in the back seat of the Maxima, squeezed between Gary Manning and Rafael Encizo.

He watched as Katz turned inside the phone booth to face the car and shrugged.

Kurtzman was having trouble cracking into the CIA's intel files. James didn't know the details, but it had something to do with the spooks hiring some new computer expert.

Katz pressed the phone against his head again. James watched him frown, nod to the receiver, say something, then hang up.

The Israeli started toward the car, then returned to the booth. When he came back, he had a Turku phone book in his hand. Sliding in on the passenger's side, he turned and rested his arm across the back seat. "Still waiting."

"Damn," Encizo said. "I've never seen Bear this stumped before."

Katz shrugged. "Aaron's good. Actually he's the best. But there are other computer experts who are good enough to slow him down occasionally. We'll call back in a few hours. In the meantime we have plenty to keep us occupied."

McCarter pulled the Maxima away from the curb. James sat back, closing his eyes.

Katz was right. The warriors of Phoenix Force wouldn't be letting any grass grow under their feet while they waited for Kurtzman to locate Dag Vaino. They had to rearm. And wherever Vaino was, he'd be protected, which meant they had to seriously rearm.

That would take time. But it would also take thought and planning.

McCarter turned a corner and Katz lifted the phone book. He squinted in the darkness, waiting until they'd passed under a streetlight to speak. "We need to find 1452 South Tegnergaten," he said. "Here." He pulled a street map of Turku from his coat and spread it across the seat.

McCarter looked down, then turned left.

Five minutes later, the Maxima slowed and drove through a residential section on the inland edge of the city. The one-story frame houses were old but well kept, the lawns as neatly manicured as putting greens. McCarter slowed further, and James saw the darkened house on the corner.

Larger than the ones they'd just passed, the home included an addition built sometime after the original structure. The wing jutted off the frame toward the side street. A large wooden sign had been erected on the roof. James couldn't read the Finnish words, but the cartoon dog on crutches, and the cat with the thermometer in his mouth, conveyed the nature of the cottage-industry business.

Whoever lived in the residential part of the structure was also a veterinarian.

McCarter circled the block and stopped. James got out.

Katz grabbed his arm through the open window as the former SEAL started to turn away. "You know what we need. Get it, and get out. Start walking back toward town. We'll pick you up."

James nodded.

As the Maxima pulled away, the Phoenix Force warrior crept silently through the backyard of the house behind the clinic, stopping at a short wooden fence.

Across the alley he could see the rear walls of both the living area and the clinic wing. A short hall connected the home to the business. A dim yard light had been attached to the top of a short pole in the center of the grass, casting a dull eerie glow over the rear of the house. But the windows were dark.

James vaulted the fence and hurried across the alley. Jumping another, similar structure, he sprinted past the light post to the rear entrance of the clinic wing.

There would be little threat once he entered the house. Even if the vet had a gun, James felt sure he could disarm the man without causing any bodily harm. But if one of the neighbors saw him breaking in, and called the police while he was still inside...

James had experienced all he wanted to of the Finnish police. And therein lay the rub, he thought as he approached the back door. He had no intention of hurting innocents, cops or civilians, which limited him severely.

So like Katz had said, he needed to get in, get out and *get gone*.

He dropped to one knee at the clinic door, fishing the glass cutter and a roll of tape out of his pocket. The tool screeched across the window in the top half of the door, and from somewhere down the block came the bark of a small dog.

James stopped cutting and listened. He heard no barks, hisses or other animal noises inside, and breathed a sigh of relief. There had been nothing on the sign to indicate that the vet boarded pets as well as treated them, and for that he was grateful. He didn't relish the thought of entering the building to suddenly find himself amid a chorus of startled pets.

James pressed several strips of tape across the window, then tapped the glass beneath it with the steel ball on the grip of the cutter. A fist-size square popped out into his hand. Reaching through the window, he twisted the lock.

A sudden sound at the rear of the house next door broke the stillness of the night. A door opening? James couldn't tell, and he couldn't wait to find out. He slipped into the vet clinic and closed the door silently behind him.

The black Phoenix Force warrior found himself inside the examining room. He stopped again, listening. Through the open door to the hall, he heard soft, feminine snoring.

James turned and twisted the head of the tiny flashlight he'd borrowed from Encizo's Swiss Army pouch. The beam fell on a gleaming metal examining table. Waist-high shelves scattered with equipment lined the walls. At the back of the room he saw what he was looking for.

The medicine cabinets.

As he started across the room toward the cabinets, the patter of feet outside the door met his ears.

Someone was running softly across the lawn.

James heard a key in the lock. His eyes darted through the room looking for cover. The cabinets were too shallow, the shelves too high to afford concealment.

As the doorknob began to twist, James killed the flashlight beam and slid beneath the examining table, pressing his back against the wall.

The door opened slowly, stopping each time the ancient wood creaked. Then a foot stepped tentatively onto the tile and the door closed.

James frowned. It was as if whoever had entered the examining room had no more desire to be discovered than he did. A burglar?

Slowly the Phoenix Force warrior leaned forward, resting his cheek against the cold tile. In the semidark room, next to the door, he saw the swollen ankles of an overweight woman. Bulging blood veins ran from her pudgy feet up her calves to wrinkled flesh hanging over her knees.

He could see no higher. And he didn't want to.

Another set of soft footsteps now padded down the hall, barely audible above the soft snores that still came from the other part of the house. James saw another set of calves, this pair snow-white and painfully thin, step into the room. They wore brown house slippers and black socks.

The voice of a middle-aged woman whispered, "Jorgen."

"Dagmar," an elderly man whispered back.

The door to the hall closed quietly.

The two sets of calves suddenly flew toward each other. James watched a faded floral-print flannel nightgown fall to the floor as stifled gasps filled the room. A pajama top, then matching shorts fell next to the gown.

The slippers and socks stayed on.

Muffled moans filled the room mixed with Finnish words James didn't understand. The woman's breathing came in fast, labored pants. The Phoenix Force warrior turned his face away from the noise and stared at the wooden baseboard at the bottom of the wall.

A moment later, there was a break in the pandemonium. Then James heard the metal table above him squeak. His hand fell instinctively to the pistol shoved into his belt as he turned back toward the vet and his lover. Two sets of calves next to the table.

Then the feet rose out of sight and the metal table began screaming in short, rhythmic shrieks.

The moans turned to gasps of pleasure. Then the stainless-steel table above James suddenly stopped threatening to snap in two, and soft sobbing whimpers were the only sounds that met Calvin James's ears.

A moment later, the calves returned to the floor. A few whispered words were spoken, then the woman slipped back into her nightgown and disappeared out the door.

The vet put his pajamas back on and crept back down the hall.

James waited until the vet's hoarse snores had joined those of his wife before crawling from beneath the table. He glanced at the glowing hands of his watch as he hurried to the medicine cabinets. Katz and the others would be wondering what had happened to him by now.

The former Navy SEAL opened the medicine cabinet and began rummaging through its contents. He found what he wanted in a drawer near the floor. Shoving the twin tranquilizer guns and two boxes of darts into his shirt, he slipped out the back door, vaulted the fence and sprinted away down the alley.

THE TUPOLEV BLACKJACK bombers streaked closer as the Executioner sprinted toward the LAV-25. "Get us into the trees!" he shouted as he dropped through the hatch.

The driver gunned the engine and threw the vehicles into gear, the Allison transmission whining as the LAV shot forward.

Bolan took a seat at the command station. He heard a cough behind him and turned to see an S.H. infantryman whose name tag read Terskol.

"You have business here, Terskol?" the Executioner growled.

The soldier cleared his throat. "I am here to serve as...as..." He faltered for the word.

The communications officer seated next to Bolan helped him out. "He's our guide, Colonel. He's the only man on board who knows the forest paths that lead to the cave."

Bolan nodded to him, then turned back to the communications officer. "Get Markus on the line," he said, pointing to the cellular telephone. "Radar should have picked up those Jacks ten minutes ago. I want to know why we weren't notified." He ripped the radio mike from the clip and spoke again. "Field Command to Larsborg Base Comm."

"Comm, sir," came back over the airwaves. Bolan recognized the voice as that of a Marine Captain Billyou.

"Billyou, we've got Tupolevs up to our ears out here. I want a squadron of F-15s in the air, I want them there *now* and I want to know why we got no advance warning."

Static filled the airways for a moment, then Billyou came back with a nervous edge to his voice. "A dozen Eagles just took off headed your way, sir. General

Markus ordered them himself—he was at Radar Control when they picked up the Tups on-screen.''

Bolan clenched his jaw. As usual, Markus had done his duty, simply throwing in a small monkey wrench along the way. His order had been delayed just long enough to ensure that it would be ineffective. The Executioner looked up to the LAV's front directional screen. They were nearing the woods.

The communications man next to the Executioner hung up the cellular phone. ''No answer at Markus's office, sir.''

''Try Radar Control,'' Bolan growled, knowing the general would be gone by now. By design.

Bolan dropped the radio back into the clip and stared at the trees on the monitor screen as the LAV raced toward cover. The cellular phone suddenly rang, and he grabbed it from the radioman's hand.

''This is Markus. We have just spotted several—''

Bolan hung up, fighting the anger that threatened to distract him from the task at hand. His attention became focused suddenly as the LAV suddenly rocked on its wheels, reacting to the concussion of a nearby explosion.

The Executioner checked the rear screen and saw a flaming Abrams tank, bombers streaking above it. ''Stop at the edge of the trees,'' he ordered the driver.

The young man glanced curiously his way, his fright evident on his face. But he did as he was told.

''Get the barrels up,'' the Executioner told the gunners on the other side of the station. Gears ground within the LAV as the men obeyed orders. ''Now, shoot them out of the sky.''

The gunner behind the controls of the 25 mm Bushmaster studied the screen, adjusted, then pressed his button. The Executioner watched an incoming Blackjack disintegrate on the monitor. But he knew the shot had been lucky. The LAV might be equipped with state-of-the-art technology, but the Soviet Union's Tupolevs hadn't been far behind when the Union fell apart. If the LAV stayed where it was, sooner or later, they'd take a hit.

Dull thuds penetrated the LAV's armored walls as a nearby tank fired toward the sky. A second Tup burst into flames on the screen. Others escaped the fire and raced past overhead.

The Executioner knew he had a decision to make. If the LAV stayed in the fight, it would soon go down like the Abrams. But if they ran to the concealment of the trees, several more of the American tanks might well fall to the Tupolevs before the F-15s arrived.

The warrior would fight on. He wouldn't allow the brave men inside the tanks to die without doing everything he could to prevent it.

Two more tanks blew to bits as the Tupolevs made another pass. The LAV took out one, but the Soviet bombers seemed to breed upon the destruction, and the screen looked no clearer than it had before.

Then, in the top left-hand corner of the monitor, the Executioner saw what at first appeared to be a swarm of bees. But he knew what they were, and he breathed a silent sigh of relief for the men in the Abrams.

The Eagles had arrived.

The screens—front, back and sides—lighted up like the fires of hell as the American fighter planes joined the skirmish. One by one, the enemy aircraft fell burning from the sky.

Bolan turned to the driver. "Get us into the trees, now. The planes can take it from here."

The soldier nodded and started out.

The Executioner glanced at the rear screen. A lone speck suddenly grew bigger as one of the last Tups raced toward them, an F-15 Eagle in hot pursuit.

An even smaller speck fell from the Blackjack a moment before it passed over the LAV.

The Soviet aircraft appeared on the forward screen, the Eagle hot on its heels. Then suddenly the Tupolev exploded. The American plane turned back, fell into formation with the rest of the squadron and started back to base.

The speck neared the LAV, then disappeared.

Bolan waited for the explosion, wondering if he would hear it before he died. When it didn't come, he glanced curiously back to the screen. Empty.

A second later what sounded like a sudden cloudburst of rain fell over the LAV, and Bolan automatically looked at the roof.

He knew immediately that the Tupolev had dropped a radioactive paint bomb on the personnel carrier.

The LAV had been marked.

The vehicle raced into the trees and started down a trail toward the caves, Terskol directing the driver through a confusing labyrinth of twists and turns. Small saplings and tree branches snapped to the sides of the LAV as it sped by.

Bolan glanced at the screens a final time as an F-15 Eagle blew the last of the Tupolevs out of the sky. That wouldn't make much difference now. With a

FLIR-equipped plane, Stensvik could trace the LAV through the brush as if it stood naked in front of the world.

The Executioner thought of the caves ahead.

The LAV's only chance.

GARY MANNING COULD HEAR Encizo breathing quietly next to him as the two men squatted in the shadows next to the school building. Fifty yards away, across the street, he saw the fifteen-foot chain-link fence circling a Turku transport company.

A waist-high hedge followed the outside of the fence, separating it from the street. Pleasant to look at, stupid from a security standpoint, Manning thought.

Good for Phoenix Force.

On the other side of the fence and hedge, parked on the gravel lot, Manning saw two dozen mammoth tractor trailer units. Beyond the trucks was a darkened, corrugated metal office building. A tiny lighted guard shack stood off to the left.

Manning watched the guard inside the shack. In his late sixties or early seventies, the man wore a chocolate-brown Eisenhower jacket and khaki eight point cap with a silver badge on the crown. His face and nose were flushed the bright red that comes from half a century of alcohol consumption.

He sat behind a desk, literally twiddling his thumbs in boredom.

"Doesn't look too tough to me," Encizo whispered.

Manning nodded in the darkness. "We can probably get one of the trucks started before the old boy even knows we're on the grounds. Drive through the gate and be gone before he realizes what's happened.''

"Then let's get it done," Encizo said. Rising to his feet, he pulled a small set of bolt cutters from his hip pocket and held them close to his side as they crept across the playground and street.

The two warriors dropped down between the fence and hedge. As the Cuban began snipping the chain links near the ground, Manning looked back to the guard shack. The old man stood and looked nervously through the window.

Manning reached out and grabbed Encizo's arm. "Wait."

A second later, the guard sat back down. With another nervous glance through the glass, he pulled a pint bottle from the inside pocket of his jacket and lifted it to his lips.

"Go on," the big Canadian told Encizo. "He didn't see us. It's just cocktail hour."

Encizo finished with the bolt cutters, then the two men crawled under the fence, rose to all fours and kept close to the ground until the guard shack disappeared from sight.

The Cuban pointed to the nearest truck. "How's this one look to you?"

"Good as any. Check the trailer and see if we need to dump anything. I'll get busy on the starter."

Encizo disappeared at the rear of the truck. Manning climbed the steps, slid behind the wheel and rolled down the window, grinning when he saw the keys in the ignition.

The transport company was putting a little too much trust in their fence and guard.

Suddenly the click of a pistol hammer cocking grabbed Manning's attention. He turned to see the old guard weaving toward him, gripping a rusty Bergmann-Baynard 9 x 23 mm automatic in both fists.

He stopped three feet from the cab and said something in Finnish.

Manning raised his hands and stuck them through the window where the guard could see them. The last thing he needed right now was to be shot by some inebriated old man whose nervous finger pulled the trigger.

The guard spoke again. His eyes closed briefly and he burped, then jerked as if trying to keep from falling asleep.

The big Canadian shook his head. "English?"

The old man's eyes narrowed to sleepy slits. He nodded. "Do not..." He burped again, then frowned, his drunken brain searching for the word. "Don't..."

Manning saw Encizo creep up behind the man. The Cuban pulled the bolt cutters from his jacket as he walked softly across the gravel. Shoving the grip against the back of the old man's head, he said, "Move. The phrase you're looking for is 'don't move.'"

The guard froze.

Encizo reached around the man and took the Bergmann-Baynard, then spun the guard toward him. The old man burped again.

Manning dropped down from the cab. "You suppose he called the cops already?"

His question was answered by the patrol car that suddenly appeared at the front gate.

Manning grabbed the guard by the shoulders and stuck his nose against the old man's. "Okay," he growled. "The cops are here. You're going to tell them it was a false alarm. You understand?" He shook the man by the shoulders.

He got no response, so shook the guard harder. The odor of stale aquavit assaulted his sinuses.

"You tell the cops your call was a false alarm—you mistook two drivers for burglars. We'll be in the truck warming up the engine. You mess up, and we'll shoot you through the window."

The guard's eyelids suddenly shot up like window blinds. He nodded.

The Phoenix Force warriors climbed into the cab as the two patrol cars drove across the gravel toward them. The guard turned his back to the truck and stood stiffly, waiting.

Manning twisted the key, and the big diesel jumped to life.

Encizo turned to him as the squad car rolled to a halt just outside the window. "We can't shoot the old boy. So you got any idea what we're going to do if he gives us up?"

Manning shrugged. "Die, I guess."

A young officer stepped from the police car and walked up to the guard. They spoke briefly, then the cop glanced up at the cab.

The big Canadian pointed down at the guard, then lifted an imaginary bottle. He tipped it to his mouth, smiled, shook his head, then shrugged.

The young cop grinned and nodded, then got back in his car.

Manning and Encizo were out of the truck as soon as the patrol car left the gate. They grabbed the old man by the arms and walked him back to the guard shack. He started to snore as the Phoenix Force warriors dropped him in his chair.

Encizo found a roll of duct tape in the desk and taped the man's ankles together. The guard came to before the Cuban could secure his hands.

"Please," the gray-haired man slurred. "Wait." He reached into his jacket and pulled out the bottle. While Manning and McCarter waited, he chugged the rest of the aquavit, then smiled. "It will be a long night," he said as he held out his hands.

Manning wrapped them, then tore off a strip and covered the guard's mouth. The old man was snoring again by the time he finished.

9

Franzen Stensvik lifted the receiver of his telephone and tapped a button.

"Yes, sir?"

"The call I have been expecting has not come?"

"I am sorry, sir," the voice said. "No."

Stensvik slammed the phone down and marched out the door into the hall. The first attack of the war hadn't gone as well as he had hoped. Yes, his bombers had destroyed several oil fields, and the castle in Larsborg had been penetrated.

But General Markus's troops had arrived before his forces could kill the bitch who ran South Haakovia. And that American bastard—what had his intelligence agents said his name was, Pollock?—had escaped as well.

No, the first battle of the war hadn't gone as well as he'd hoped. But all wasn't lost. He still had several hole cards to play. And the first centered around the phone call he was expecting.

Three floors down, Stensvik strutted importantly into the conference room. The faces seated at the long rectangular table were Japanese, and he felt a moment of revulsion at the sight of the misshapen eyes and yellow skin. Small. Short. Even shorter than he himself. Perhaps that was what allowed him to stomach them.

Naoto Sasamori, chief executive officer of the Hagakure Corporation, had come himself, and now the man and his underlings rose to their feet, bowing their respect. Stensvik nodded back and took a seat at the head of the table. He decided to get right to the point. "Why have you come?"

The short, stocky Japanese was visibly taken aback by the rudeness, which made Stensvik smile. He watched the man drop back into his chair, his eyes on the table. "Stensvik-san," he said in a low, gravelly voice, "we must discuss the new situation."

"What is there to discuss? It is simple. We have a deal—you agreed to supply me with enough money to fight a war in exchange for the oil-drilling rights in South Haakovia. Nothing has changed."

"But Stensvik-san," Sasamori politely protested, "you assured us the war would be over in hours. It was not. And your losses have been far greater than we expected."

"You gambled," Stensvik said simply. "And you lost more than you intended to. Forget it. When the war is over, you will drill for oil in both North *and* South Haakovia. Now, as long as you are here, I need more money."

Again, the shock showed on Sasamori's face. Then his eyes narrowed behind his thick black glasses and he said softly, "No."

Stensvik forced himself to wait, in spite of his mounting anger. If he had learned anything about the Japanese since they'd come to him begging for drilling rights, it was that they were a shrewd race of people. They always had a plan of attack.

"We will be part of this no longer," Sasamori said nervously. "And without our money, you will soon suffer defeat."

Stensvik smiled. Was that their battle plan? This would be easier than he'd thought.

The North Haakovian president stood and clasped his hands behind his back. Head down, he paced back and forth across the room, using the time to phrase in his mind what he was about to say. He wanted his words to have the ultimate impact when he said them.

Finally he returned to the table and stood next to his chair. He allowed his face to relax, then said quietly, "I am sorry you feel that way. Sorry for the Hagakure Corporation, but even more sorry for the people of Japan as a whole."

There was a moment of silence, then the men around the conference table turned to one another, wondering what this could mean.

Stensvik cleared his throat to show he hadn't finished. "I admit that you are correct, Sasamori-san. Without money to replace weapons and parts, I will soon suffer defeat. But even in defeat, victory will be mine."

More whispers around the table. Then Sasamori said, "Please explain."

Stensvik's face took on a blank expression as he voiced the words he had rehearsed in his brain a moment before. "You are correct, but only partially so," he said in a quiet, even tone as if reading off his shopping list. "But you have ignored the consequences of my defeat."

Sasamori and the other Japanese businessmen waited.

"If my conventional attack is not successful, I will be forced to resort to unconventional methods. Nuclear and chemical weapons. Already I have distributed sarin and soman nerve agents across the world. North Haakovian operatives are standing by, ready to release them as soon as I give the order." He paused to let it sink in, then went on. "There are enough chemicals in Japan at the moment to reduce your population by fifty percent."

The faces around the table seemed to pale.

Stensvik allowed himself a chuckle. "And the other fifty percent, you wonder?" he said. "Why, the rather large nuclear missiles presently aimed at Tokyo should take care of them nicely."

A young man sitting to Sasamori's right drew in a shocked breath. The thin Japanese in a blue suit on the CEO's other side suddenly gagged.

Stensvik waited for them to regain control. The last line he had come up with was his favorite, and he wanted to time it perfectly.

When the men around the table had recaptured their composure, Franzen Stensvik stood erect and threw back his chest importantly. Then, placing his right hand inside his coat, he tapped his hip with the riding crop and said, "Tokyo is not alone. I have other warheads aimed at your islands. All major cities except Nagasaki and Hiroshima." He paused, letting the horror sink in, then finished. "I still respect you gentlemen, and for that reason I have decided to allow those two cities to remain intact. After all, they have already been practically bombed out of existence once this century.''

The expressions of the younger Hagakure executives seated around the table went blank. But on the faces of those old enough to remember, Franzen Stensvik saw the terror he had intended his words to produce. Without another word he turned and left the room.

A tall slender soldier wearing captain's bars hurried to his side as he reached the elevator. The man held an open attaché case in his hands. Stensvik saw the cellular phone.

''The call you have been waiting for,'' the captain said. ''It has come.''

Stensvik grabbed the phone from the man's hand and pressed it to his ear. ''You have thought about what we discussed?'' he said without formalities.

''Yes.''

''And your answer?''

''Yes.''

By the time the elevator doors opened again, Stensvik had hung up and was cackling in pleasure.

CARL LYONS GAZED wearily from the Cessna as Charlie Mott dropped the plane over Stony Man Mountain. The green forests of hardwoods and conifers below looked peaceful, and the ex-LAPD detective felt fatigue fall over him like a cloak. He closed his eyes, floating in the semiconsciousness that comes just before sleep.

The Cessna's wheels hit the tarmac and jerked the Able Team leader back to attention. He turned to the window as they raced along the runway. The bulging chin and Roman nose of the "old man" of Stony Man Mountain flashed by.

Lyons heard snoring behind him and turned to see both Gadgets and Pol fast asleep. His eyes glided back to the window as Mott brought the plane to a halt. Ahead lay the main house.

The radio scratched and Barbara Price's voice came over the airwaves. "Base to Able."

He lifted the microphone to his lips. "Yeah, Barb."

"Hal's here. Report to the war room."

"Damn," he heard Pol's sleepy voice say behind him.

"No rest for the wicked," Schwarz mumbled.

"Yeah, but we're supposed to be the good guys," Pol replied.

Lyons dropped down from the plane and led his men across the ground to the front door. He slipped a card into the security lock, then tapped in the code. A hidden panel swung back near the knob to reveal a small frame of glass. He pressed his left thumb against it, then punched another series of numbers into the lock.

The steel door buzzed, then swung open.

The men of Able Team hurried into the entryway and descended the steps to the basement. Another series of codes got them into the war room, where Hal Brognola stood next to a six-foot television screen. He wore a wrinkled charcoal-gray suit. His white shirt looked as if he'd slept in it as well, and his red rep tie had been unknotted and hung loosely around his neck.

"Grab a seat," the Justice man growled, his hoarse voice giving away the fact that he'd been existing on coffee and seldom-smoked cigars.

Lyons and company dropped into the chairs in front of the screen.

Brognola pushed a button on the videotape player beneath the set, and a series of numbers flashed by. Then the face of an elderly, harsh-looking Oriental wearing a light cotton suit and sunglasses appeared.

"No sound?" Blancales asked.

"They got it, but it's poor quality," Brognola said. "The mumbling's been magnified and deciphered, but we haven't had time yet to add the cleaned-up track to the picture. I'll give you what's important as we go."

The camera lens moved back to show the gray-haired Oriental walking down a crowded street. The man's gait defied his apparent age as he moved lithely past storefronts lettered with Chinese characters.

"Recognize the face?" Brognola asked.

Schwarz responded as quick as a game-show contestant. "Bin Chou," he said. "Benny to his friends . . . if he had any."

"Red Chinese Intel, right?" Blancanales added.

"Correct," Brognola said.

Chou entered a dimly lighted café. There was a two-second break while the tape went dark, then the Chinese appeared again, sitting at a table. There was just enough difference in the two tapes to convince Lyons that the surveillance inside was being done by another camera.

"This come from the CIA?" the Able Team leader asked.

"Right first time," Brognola said. "Kurtzman finally broke their new computer man's codes for Phoenix Force. And when he did, he opened up a whole new can of worms. Besides info on Vaino's HQ in Finland, he got this."

A tall, muscular Caucasian joined Chou at his table, his face away from the camera. A waitress took their order, and when she departed they began to speak.

"What are they saying?" Schwarz asked.

"Small talk right now. How's the wife and kids. Just wait."

The camera—most likely hidden in a briefcase—bobbed up and down as the CIA agent operating it slowly began to maneuver around the room, trying to get an angle on the Caucasian's face. A moment later, it stopped again and a sharp nose on the front of an almost perfectly round Slavic head appeared on the screen.

"Rikkard Donskoy," Lyons said. "He's KGB."

Brognola smiled. "*Was* KGB, Ironman. After the collapse he went with Stensvik."

"So what the hell are these two doing together?" Pol wanted to know. "The last report we had, Red China wasn't even on speaking terms with Stensvik."

"Things change," Brognola replied. "The Communists of the world have become a dying breed, and those who are still around are bonding in the hopes they won't become an extinct species."

Chou looked around the café quickly, then leaned forward.

Brognola glanced down at a typed page of notes on the table in front of him. "Right now they're talking about the situation in Beijing. Chou says something to the effect that the graybeard isolationists in power are about to die off. When they do, a more progressive and worldly regime will take over. Now Donskoy asks how long he thinks that will take, and Chou answers that it probably won't take as long as the chairman thinks."

On-screen, both men laughed politely.

"Chinese Intel's going to knock off the old man?" Gadgets asked.

Brognola shrugged. "Sounds like that's what they've got planned."

"Then Stensvik and Chou are forming an alliance behind the scenes," Lyons said. "Just in case. Even if the chairman doesn't go down, he can't live forever, and the young bucks who'll be coming into power in the next few years want a head start on things. Things like the oil everybody knows the Japanese are after in Sorth Haakovia."

"And don't forget the Haakovias border Russia," Pol added. "How far is Saint Petersburg, maybe thirty miles? It wouldn't hurt to have a base just north of the border in case those two age-old enemies go toe-to-toe again sometime."

"You've both hit the nail on the head." Brognola rattled the page in his hand. "Maybe I should just throw this thing away and shut up."

Chou and Donskoy continued to converse on-screen. Finally the former KGB operative leaned forward again, his face a mask of intense concentration.

"Here's the bottom line," Brognola said. "The Colombians bungled the assassinations at the UN. The job's now being farmed out to the Chinese. If Chou's men can take out the South Haakovian diplomats, they can have the drilling rights."

"The same rights Stensvik promised to the Japanese," Blancanales observed.

"So we're heading back to the General Assembly," Lyons said. "How soon? We got time to sack out for a while?"

Brognola didn't answer. The tape went black again, then came back on.

Another camera. This time the scene was an airport customs booth. The officers wore United States flag shoulder patches.

"Washington, D.C.," Brognola announced.

Benny Chou, sporting the same black sunglasses and light cotton suit, extended a passport. A customs man stamped it, and he passed through the turnstile.

"Guess the answer to the shut-eye is no," Gadgets said.

Lyons rose from his chair and walked toward the door.

"Grab forty winks on the plane," he heard Brognola say as he led his team from the room.

SPORADIC SUNLIGHT shot through the trees of the dense forest, casting spotlights of white on the LAV as it raced down the trail toward the caves.

Bolan sat at the command station, watching the screen in front of his face, which showed the tops of the darkened pines and the blue patches of sky beyond.

The Executioner didn't know what the Soviets had named their version of the U.S. Martin Marietta Low-Altitude Navigation Targeting InfraRed Night (LANTIRN) system. But he knew that equipped with the Soviet version of FLIR imagery, it did the same thing.

In the attack phase the pod sensors automatically fixed the position of their targets, then identified and categorized those targets before passing the information to the fire-control system.

The system then fired laser-guided munitions.

The North Haakovian plane, when it arrived, would be a flying, shooting robot that made no mistakes. The LAV's only chance was the shelter of the caves.

The Executioner didn't have to wonder whether General Markus would send the Eagles back. He would.

But they would be just a little bit late.

"To the right," Terskol's heavily accented voice said behind the Executioner. The driver followed the Haakovian's order, whipping the vehicle onto a side trail.

More trees flew by, more bushes and limbs fell along the sides of the trail. They slowed the progress of the personnel carrier, but Bolan thanked the stars for their presence anyway. While the tracker plane would be able to pinpoint them within the forest if it caught them before the caves, the heavy foliage might help deflect the lasers. Maybe.

But the Executioner didn't kid himself. Sooner or later, a beam would slip down through an opening just like the sun rays that made it all the way to the needle-covered forest floor.

Bolan turned toward the Marine lieutenant driving the LAV. Terskol had moved in to his side and now stood bracing himself on the back of the lieutenant's seat. "Left," the Haakovian said. "It is only a kilometer or so more—"

A flash of light suddenly drew the Executioner's eyes to the rear screen. He saw the trees directly behind them burst into flames.

The driver accelerated. Branches and leaves flew in a whirlwind as the armored car sliced through them like a machete. Then the forward screen suddenly turned white. The picture returned a moment later, and Bolan saw that the trees ahead were now burning.

The tracker plane had positioned them. And the pilot was smart. He would stop their forward motion, then fire down into the area between the two fires until his missiles hit their mark.

"Left," the Haakovian guide screamed as they came to another side trail. The lieutenant whipped the LAV onto the narrow path and immediately rammed the thick trunk of a towering pine.

Bolan and the driver jerked forward in their seats. The Haakovian slammed up against the instrument panel, his head striking a knob with the sickening thump of a melon hitting the ground. He slithered to the floor.

The tall pine tree snapped, but the LAV ground to a halt.

"Back it out!" Bolan yelled as more fire lighted up the forest to their side. He unstrapped his safety belt and reached down, grabbing the Haakovian by the shoulders and lifting him to his feet. Blood oozed from a contusion on the man's temple. The warrior released him, and Terskol slumped back to the floor, his eyes opened wide in death.

Bolan turned to the lieutenant as they started back down the trail. "You know the way?"

The man swallowed hard as he shook his head.

The LAV raced blindly on, taking side trails each time they appeared. The forest fires around them spread until the Executioner could feel their heat through the vehicles' thick steel walls. The screens—all of them, front, aft and both sides—were masses of flames.

The LAV drove through the fire, the inside temperature rising. Sweat soaked Bolan's shirt and rolled down his face as the personnel carrier threatened to become an oven and roast the men inside alive.

Then suddenly, the screen ahead of them cleared. Bolan watched as the LAV shot out of the trees. The Executioner saw several burned-out Abrams tanks in the clearing. The driver had unwittingly taken the same trail on which they'd entered the forest and circled back.

The lieutenant leaned hard on the brake, trying to slow enough to U-turn back into the trees. On the left screen the Executioner saw the Soviet tracker plane appear. It flew slowly their way, closing until even the red hammer-sickle-and-fish insignia on its wings became visible.

Bolan sat back, awaiting the inevitable as the driver continued to fight the wheel. The LAV seemed to turn in slow motion as the North Haakovian aircraft flew confidently forward.

They would never make it.

Then the screen turned white again. An explosion rocked the LAV to its core. When the vehicle finally settled, the screen lighted up again. The Soviet tracker lay two hundred yards away on the ground, fires shooting up from its devastated metal skeleton.

A familiar voice came over on the radio.

"Hey, big guy," Jack Grimaldi said. "Just happened to be in the neighborhood. Thought maybe you could use a hand."

Grimaldi's Lockheed F-104 Starfighter flew past the screen, dipping a wing as if tipping its hat, and was gone.

YAKOV KATZENELENBOGEN hung up the phone and chuckled. He was happy for two reasons. First, Kurtzman had hit the jackpot when he finally broke through the new CIA entry code. Info less than twenty-four hours old pinpointed Dag Vaino's armed compound in the woods just north of Helsinki.

Katz stood up from the seat inside the phone booth and gazed across the street at the second reason for his good humor. Security around the Turku police headquarters was lax. Practically nonexistent. And after all of the unexpected stumbling blocks Phoenix Force had encountered during this mission into Finland, that fact pleased Yakov Katzenelenbogen more than he could have expressed.

He moved out of the phone booth to the low retaining wall in front of the city offices. Through the glass front door of the police station, he could see a waiting room. Across the room, in the far wall, was another door, closed. The corner of the information window to one side extended just into his field of vision, and every few seconds a blue uniform sleeve moved into the picture. The arm inside the sleeve appeared to be writing.

To the right of the building was a fenced-in parking lot. Through the chain links of the fence, the former

Mossad agent could see six squad cars parked in a neat row. Farther to the right were two helipads. One was vacant, but the other was occupied by a small two-seater, four-blade Hughes helicopter.

A lone squad car had been parked in the slanted spaces in front of the building. It was the one on which Katz, and the rest of Phoenix Force, now waited.

The door against the far wall of the waiting room opened. Katz caught a glimpse of an orange plastic table filled with ashtrays in the room behind. A squad room.

Two blue-uniformed policemen strode out the door, crossed the waiting room and exited the building. The lead officer, tall and broad-shouldered, stopped next to the driver's side of the car.

Katzenelenbogen stood up behind the wall and shot him in the chest as he stuck a key into the lock. James stepped out of the shadows to the side of the building and put a quick round between the shoulder blades of the cop's partner as the man reached for the handle on the passenger's side.

Manning, Encizo and McCarter appeared behind James and dragged the limp forms back around the corner into the alley. Katz hurried to their sides. James knelt and shoved an index finger onto the throats of both cops, checking their pulse.

''They're fine,'' the black Phoenix Force warrior whispered, reloading the tranquilizer gun. ''They'll just sleep it off here, then wonder how they ended up in the alley in their underwear.''

Katz reloaded the other tranquilizer pistol and stuck it back under his shirt. The rest of the team dropped to the asphalt and began disrobing the two men.

"Who gets to play cops?" Manning asked.

James grinned at Encizo, then looked back to Manning. "You and McCarter are the two most WASPy-looking," he teased.

Encizo chuckled as he removed one of the men's boots.

McCarter snorted. He stopped unbuttoning a tunic long enough to say, "The Finns might be white, but they're not Anglo-Saxons. Historians think—"

"Can you believe this?" James complained. "Just put on a uniform, Mr. Brit. You're the closest thing to a Finn we've got."

A minute later, McCarter and Manning wore the uniforms of a Finnish police sergeant and patrolman.

"Guess that makes us the robbers," Encizo said. He, Katz and James clasped their hands together behind their backs to simulate being handcuffed. McCarter and Manning shoved them back down the alley, around the corner and through the front door. They passed a set of rest rooms in the opposite wall and walked purposefully toward the info desk.

The desk sergeant at the window looked up as the five men walked in. He stared at McCarter and Manning, and it was clear that he was wondering why he didn't recognize them.

That brief hesitation was all Phoenix Force got—but it was what they had counted on. And more than enough. As the expression of confusion faded on the Finnish cop's face, and his hand shot toward his holster, Katz whipped the tranquilizer gun from under his shirt and fired another "sleeper" round through the window.

He was already reloading the weapon as the sergeant slumped over his desk.

James hurried to the window and stuck his head through the opening. Past the info desk, he saw an office area running the side of the building, front to back. Several cubicle offices had been constructed with pasteboard dividers, and a large bull pen of a dozen more desks rested against the rear wall.

The bull pen was empty, but James couldn't tell about the tiny cubicles. Turning around, he whispered his findings to the rest of the team.

"Take a look," Katz whispered back. "Take Gary with you. David, you, Rafael and I will take the squad room."

James and Manning crawled through the window as McCarter, wearing the sergeant's stripes, opened the door. He stepped into the room and smiled, holding the door open.

Katz saw two fingers extended on the hand that braced the door. He drew the tranquilizer gun.

The man sitting behind the orange table smoking a pipe never moved. At least not until the tranquilizer dart pierced his neck and he fell forward.

But the second Finn, wearing captain's bars on the lapel of his uniform blouse, jumped to his feet. McCarter drew the pistol from his holster and pointed it between the policeman's eyes.

The captain got the message. He stared in frozen shock as Katz reloaded the tranquilizer gun, aimed and fired.

A side door suddenly opened and Katz, McCarter and Encizo swung their weapons that way, lowering them as James and Manning entered the squad room.

"All clear," James said. He pointed toward the rear of the room. "The armory has to be somewhere back there."

Katz led his men cautiously through another door into a storage area. They passed into a short hall that eventually intersected with another corridor. A steel door, secured by a heavy padlock, stood at the junction. The Israeli led his men to the door and saw that the side passage led to the outside of the building. The parking area, and the helipads, had to be on the other side.

He turned to the padlock and shook his head in disbelief. Human beings, even trained human beings, never ceased to amaze him with their ability to overlook the obvious. The door was 10-gauge steel. The lock big, heavy, expensive. Sawing through it would take time, picking it even longer, and they might search the offices for the key all night and come up with nothing.

But the walls surrounding the door had been constructed of half-inch wallboard.

The ex-Mossad agent stepped forward and drove the butt of the tranquilizer gun through the wall between the studs. He ripped down, tearing away a large chunk, then punched through the board on the other side. Through the hole leading into the dark room, he saw the outlines of rifles.

James stepped forward to help him. Seconds later they had an opening large enough to pass through.

Katz turned to Manning. "Start at the front offices. Find the keys to the helicopter. Take one of the tranquilizer guns." As the big Canadian took off, Katz turned to McCarter and James. "Stay here. Rafael and I will pass everything out to you." He squeezed through the hole in the wall, found the light switch and flipped it on.

The rifles rested in a rack against the wall. He reached up, pulling down a Sako-Valmet M-43, and handed it to Encizo behind him. The Cuban stuck it through the hole to James, who braced it against the wall in the hallway. After passing out four more rifles, Katz moved on to a rack of Suomi Model 31 submachine guns.

The members of Phoenix Force had already picked up handguns along the way, and Katz skipped the Lahti autos he found stacked in boxes against the wall. They looked knew, untested. The warriors had no time to work out the kinks.

Encizo helped Katz pass several cases of 9 mm and 7.62 mm ammo to James's waiting hands. The Phoenix Force leader turned toward a steel box against the wall. He couldn't read the writing that labeled the top, but he could guess what the box contained—C-4 plastique, light charges, just enough to knock down doors and break through barricades. But by the time Manning was through wiring enough of them together, they'd have bombs capable of doing whatever was required.

He opened the box and carefully withdrew several smaller ones. He and Encizo had transferred them to the waiting hands in the hall, when Katz's eyes fell on a canvas tarp in the far corner of the room. "Load what we've got," he called out to McCarter and James, "and get the chopper warmed up as soon as you've got the keys." He hurried to the tarp and raised it.

The hint of a grin tugged at the corners of Katz's mouth, as he gazed at a 20 mm Lahti Model 39 anti-tank gun. He turned to Encizo. Without being told, the Cuban lifted the big gun into his arms and squeezed back through the wall. His feet tapped the tile, then Katz heard the outside door open. The Israeli found a case of ammo farther back under the tarp and ducked back through the hole to the hall.

At the sound of running footsteps in the squad room Katz dropped the ammo box and drew the tranquilizer gun. Manning darted through the door. "You want the good news, or the bad news?" the big Canadian asked.

Katz glanced at the key in Manning's hand. "I can see the good news."

Manning nodded. "The bad news is there was an officer at the front desk when I got there. I tapped him on the head, but he'd evidently put out the alert already. Three squad cars just rolled up in front with their headlights off."

Katz felt his jaws tighten. The rest rooms in the front of the building. No one had checked them. One of the cops had to have been inside.

He pointed to the anti-tank ammo on the floor. "Get out to the chopper and have David get it started." He shoved the tranquilizer gun into his pants and pulled its twin from the small of the Canadian's back.

Manning took off for the yard as more footsteps sounded in the squad room. Slow. Cautious. Katz waited.

When the steps neared the door, he threw it open, stuck the tranquilizer pistol through the opening and fired. A short overweight man fell to the floor.

Katz shoved him away from the door with a boot, dropped the empty weapon and drew the other tranquilizer gun. A young uniformed Finn with light blond hair froze in the middle of the room, giving the Israeli time to put him to sleep.

The Phoenix Force leader dropped the second tranquilizer pistol next to the first and drew the Lahti 9 mm from his belt. Another police officer appeared in the doorway to the lobby, and Katz fired high, stitching a line of gunfire over the lintel.

The man pivoted back through the door.

Katz heard the helicopter's engine kick over. Gunfire suddenly erupted from the same direction, and he squeezed the trigger again, emptying the clip into the ceiling. Turning down the hall, he sprinted to the door and dived into the yard.

The Phoenix Force leader took in the situation as he rolled to his feet. By now, six more police cars had arrived to join the three in front of the building. They stood just outside the fence, their engine blocks turned to provide cover for the cops crouched behind them. Red flames leaped over the hoods of the vehicles as the officers fired pistols and shotguns toward the helicopter.

James and Manning stood behind the tiny aircraft. The rifles in their hands bucked up and down as they peppered the police cars with rounds, carefully avoiding the cops themselves.

The front tires on one of the cars exploded and the vehicle sank to the concrete as Katz raced toward the chopper, squeezing the trigger of the recharged Lahti on the run, sending rounds high into the air. A burst of fire ate into the ground near his feet, kicking up dry clods of dirt and pebbles.

Manning turned toward Katz as he neared the chopper, ushering the man into the passenger's seat.

McCarter revved the engine as Encizo climbed in on top of Katz, taking a seat on his lap. The chopper began to rise. James and Manning looped the slings of their Valmets over the skids as the Hughes coughed, hesitated, then went airborne, pulling the two dangling men into the air.

Encizo fired a burst of 7.62 mm rounds groundward. The hot brass flew from the chamber and struck Katz in the face, their heat burning his skin. The gunfire from below continued.

McCarter leveled off, then flew over the fence. A second later they had cleared a block of houses and the shooting stopped.

Katz looked down through the door and saw that James and Manning had climbed their slings and now gripped the skids with their hands.

"Wherever we're headed, get there fast," James called up through the wind.

"Take advantage of the situation," Encizo shouted to his comrade. "Get in a few chin-ups."

Both men hanging from the chopper told him exactly what he could do with his chin-ups as they held on for dear life.

McCarter turned in his seat as he flew his teammates to safety. He glanced first at Katz, then at the little Cuban seated on the Israeli's lap. "People will say you're in love," he said dryly, then turned his eyes back to the sky.

10

Carl Lyons had never been inside the Helmsley Palace. Not on a cop's salary. But he had driven past on occasion, and the place did seem impressive. Once he was inside, Lyons couldn't believe just how luxurious and ornate the place was. Rooms 505 through 520 seemed appropriate accommodations for the South Haakovian diplomats. Again, the delegates to the UN had resisted protective custody. So if they were going to be assassinated, Lyons thought, they might as well have their brains blown out in style.

The Able Team leader reached for the microphone on the dash as Schwarz pulled the vehicle to a halt in front of the hotel. "Able One to Stony Man," he said. "We'll be leaving the vehicle at the Palace. They got our walkie-talkies upstairs?"

"That's affirmative, Ironman," Price came back. "See the agent in charge. He's waiting for you."

Lyons opened the door and got out. According to Kurtzman's latest CIA intel, Benny Chou was still in Washington. Probably rounding up an army of Red Chinese "sleeper" agents who'd been lying low in the U.S. for years and just waiting to be of such use. But Chou would show up here sooner or later, and the big ex-cop was anxious to get set up as soon as possible.

A uniformed doorman opened Schwarz's door and took the keys. The Able Team warriors exited the car and made their way into the lobby of the hotel, which they scanned as they moved across the room. Lyons's gaze landed on three men entering an elevator. They were dressed in tasteful gray and blue pin-striped suits, and he could see only the backs of the men's heads— long straight black hair on one, shorter straight black hair on the second. The third man's hair had gone a gray that almost matched his suit. He walked smoothly with an agility that contradicted the wrinkles of skin on the back of his neck.

Lyons had seen that walk before. On the videotape Brognola had shown them at the Farm.

The ex-LAPD detective instinctively moved his hand under his suitcoat to the butt of the Python as the men turned to face the front of the elevator. As the door closed, he caught a brief glimpse of the face under the gray hair.

Oriental. Sunglasses.

"Chou."

"What?" Blancanales said.

"It's Chou. Don't ask me how, but he's already here." Lyons reached for the place on his side where he always clipped walkie-talkies, then cursed when his hand met an empty belt. He turned to Blancanales, then nodded toward the registration desk. "Get on the phone and warn the agents upstairs." Pivoting toward Schwarz, he said, "Let's go."

The two men had started toward the staircase when several side doors to the lobby suddenly flew open. A group of protestors who had been picketing outside rushed into the lobby and sprinted through the room, blocking the elevators and exits, and cutting Lyons and Schwarz off from the stairs.

A bearded man carrying a hand-painted sign jerked a revolver from beneath his tattered shirt and raised it over his head. Screams echoed through the spacious lobby, then were drowned out as the bearded man pulled the trigger. "We demand your attention!" he shrieked, his eyes wild.

Lyons stopped in his tracks. One of two things was going on here. Chou had either recruited local help to create a diversion while he hit the South Haakovians, or he'd gotten lucky in his timing. The Able Team leader didn't know which had happened, and if the truth were known, he didn't give a damn.

At least one of the protestors was armed and dangerous. And they were about to be responsible for assassinations that might trigger into World War III.

Lyons turned to Schwarz. "We don't have time for this shit. Deal with it, then catch up to me." He moved toward the stairs as cries of horror continued behind him.

"Hey guy," Lyons heard Schwarz say to his rear.

A moment later, he heard a fist crack against bone. He glanced over his shoulder as he neared the stairs and saw the bearded man on the floor. Schwarz handed the revolver to one of the uniformed doormen as men Lyons assumed to be hotel detectives converged on the lobby.

Their leader down, the would-be rioters made their way hastily toward the exits.

Both Schwarz and Blancanales raced to Lyons's side as the Able Team leader opened the door to the stairs.

"I got the agent in charge on the line," Pol said, "but it went dead before the guy hung up."

Lyons didn't waste his breath answering. He nodded as he took the first flight of stairs three at a time.

Able Team had reached the third floor when the door suddenly cracked open. The barrel of an Uzi appeared in the opening and a wild spray of 9 mm parabellums saturated the hall.

Lyons dived to the concrete landing, double-actioning a .357 round from the Python as he fell. The bullet passed through the door, but the assault continued.

In the corner of his eye he saw Schwarz take a direct hit to the chest and fly back against the wall. The round tore his shirt away, revealing the ballistic nylon vest beneath the singed material. Both Lyons and Blancanales opened fire, the noise deafening in the confines of the stairwell.

The Uzi fell to the floor. The door swung open and the long-haired Oriental Lyons had seen on the elevator toppled onto the tile at his feet.

The stairwell quieted as the echoing rounds died down. Lyons turned toward Schwarz, who had already been helped to his feet by Pol. "You okay?" the ex-cop asked.

Schwarz started to nod, then Lyons saw his gaze jerk suddenly to the floor overhead. At the same instant, from below, the Able Team leader heard the click of another Uzi as the bolt slid home.

Then the gunfire began. Again.

GARY MANNING was a woodsman. He'd grown up in the wilds of the Canadian forests and had had a fishing rod and hunting rifle in his hands almost as soon as he'd been old enough to carry them. Manning loved the woods, loved the sounds, the smells, the touch of leaves against his skin and the sense of freedom he got while trekking through the trees.

But, Manning thought as he paused to wipe the perspiration from his forehead and gaze out through the darkened trees north of Helsinki, if he never saw the forests of Finland again, he might just die a happy man.

The big Canadian clipped the plastic-covered wire he held and sat up on the truck seat. He had finished wiring the trailer with explosives a half hour ago, but it had been the plastique in the tractor itself that had forced hard reality into his brain.

There was no way he could pull off the bombing attack on Vaino's headquarters and keep from dying himself. Not, at least, the way they'd planned it. If he jumped from the truck in time to save himself, there was no way to guarantee the mobile bombs would continue on course.

And there was no time to formulate an alternate plan. Dag Vaino was slippery, and another delay might mean he would escape again.

Footsteps pounded through the trees, and Rafael Encizo suddenly appeared in front of the truck. Manning watched him through the windshield as the Cuban caught his breath, then leaned through the window into the cab. "It'll work," Encizo said. "The place is concrete. My guess is the walls are at least three feet. But there's a road leading right to the front gate, and only two guard towers. The fence and the gate are probably hot, but this thing will roll right through it. Two doors. If you take out either one—"

"I'll get both," Manning said, surprised at how sharp his voice sounded.

Encizo stared at him, then nodded slowly.

The big Canadian climbed from the truck, glad that he hadn't shared the knowledge with the other men of Phoenix Force that his plan had a major flaw. They'd try to talk him out of it. At the rear of the trailer he saw Katz and James hard at work reassembling the helicopter. Knowing that radar as well as everything that flew in the skies of Finland would be searching for the stolen Hughes, it had been broken down for the ride back to Helsinki. The black Nissan Maxima had been its traveling companion in the giant truck's trailer.

A voice called out to Manning from between the tractor and trailer. "Grab the wire and pull it on through," McCarter said.

Manning lifted himself back up into the cab. He saw a stiff piece of wire catch at the top of the hole in the dash where the radio had once been. He grabbed it, pulled and took up the slack.

McCarter appeared at the open door a second later, axle grease smeared across his hands and face. "Okay," the Briton said. "From here it's simple." He handed Manning the wrench he'd been using. "Just wrap the wire around this little bugger and use it as the handle. Then pull just before you jump. The tractor and trailer should separate, and if you give the wheel a hard right at the same time, you'll have one bomb going left, the other right." McCarter's face shone with enthusiasm.

Manning's nod seemed to wipe the smile away. "Everything all right?" the Englishman asked.

Irritation flooded Manning's body. "Hey, *you* screw around for two hours with enough C-4 to blow you into vapors and see if *you're* in the mood to giggle."

Katz's hand fell on Manning's shoulder. "Some problem?"

The big Canadian shook his head. "Nah. I'm just a little uptight from the work, I guess."

Katz stared at him with the same curiosity Manning had seen on the faces of the other two Phoenix Force warriors.

Encizo and James joined them. "We ready?"

"Yes," Katz said, "but let's run through it one more time. Calvin, you, Rafael and I give Gary a one-minute head start in the truck. Then you and David take off in the chopper. David flies, Calvin mans the antitank gun. Rafael and I will cover the rear flank in the Maxima. We all wait for the boom, then move in to shoot the rats as they flee the burning ship." He turned to face Manning. "You make damn sure you get out as soon as you pull the wire. How much distance do you need between you and the building?"

Manning forced himself to shrug casually. "Hundred, maybe a hundred and fifty yards."

"Then give it two," Katz said. "That's an order."

Before he could stop himself, Manning had raised his hand to his forehead in an exaggerated salute.

"Let's go," Katz said, and he and Encizo headed to the Maxima as James and McCarter boarded the two-seater helicopter.

Manning felt hollow as he climbed up into the cab of the truck. He twisted the key and the engine roared to life. "Well, everybody has to die sometime," he said out loud.

The big Canadian guided the truck over the bumpy road, twisting through several curves. He rounded a bend and suddenly a gray concrete building appeared, maybe an eighth of a mile in the distance. He saw the two doors in the wall facing him, and leaned forward on the accelerator to pick up speed.

As the truck-bomb raced toward Dag Vaino's headquarters, Manning took comfort in the fact that his death would have meaning....

FIVE HUNDRED FEET above the treetops, Calvin James watched the tractor trailer race down the road toward Dag Vaino's compound. He thought of Manning, and the way the big Canadian had acted just before they left the clearing where they'd prepared for the attack.

Manning had been abrupt. Odd for the friendliness that usually characterized the man. But James could understand that. This mission had been hard on all of them, and not even the warriors of Phoenix Force were completely immune to stress.

No, that wasn't what bothered James. What bothered him was the look he had seen in Manning's eyes. It reminded him of something. What?

Suddenly the answer hit him, and James felt his heart pound in his chest as he stared down at the truck again. It was the look of someone who had accepted his fate—death. In a flash he understood why Manning had seemed so uptight. The big Canadian had decided that to ensure that the tractor and trailer hit their marks, he'd have to stay with them past the point of no return. He intended to give his life to guarantee that they finally got Dag Vaino. He hadn't shared this wrinkle in the plan with the other members of the team, and they had all been too busy with their own preparations to notice.

James jerked in his seat to follow the truck as it drove on. The vehicle was less than half a mile from its objective now, twisting through the curves in the road that led to the compound. He didn't know exactly how long he had to come up with a plan to save Manning and carry it out, but it wasn't long.

"Fly over the truck!" James shouted suddenly.

McCarter turned to him as if he'd lost his mind. "Katz said to stay behind it. We can't—"

James grabbed the Briton's arm. "Just do it!" he yelled above the chopping noise of the blades. "Trust me!" He swiveled in his seat toward the chopper's storage compartment directly behind the seat. "I don't have time to explain."

McCarter didn't hesitate. He kicked the Hughes forward.

The black Phoenix Force warrior turned to kneel over the seat as he sorted frantically through the cluttered equipment in the dark compartment. Police helicopters performed a variety of functions, and one of them was rescue duty. Somewhere amid the articles in the back would be what he needed.

James's hands fell onto the coiled rescue line and he jerked it over the seat. His heart leaped in his chest again as he saw the harness already attached.

Manning wouldn't have time to get into it.

The ex-SEAL looked down again as the chopper flew over the truck. Manning had rounded the last turn and had a straightaway to the compound. He was less than a quarter mile away, and speeding up.

There was only one way.

"He's not bailing out," James said as he snapped the leather straps around his waist and shoulders. In the corner of his eye he saw McCarter nod. He breathed a silent sigh of relief. McCarter had figured out what Manning was doing, too. Further communication wouldn't be necessary. He'd know what to do.

"How long's the line?" the Briton asked.

James glanced at the coil. "Hundred feet, I'm guessing," he replied as he stood.

"Let's hope you're right," he heard McCarter say as he leaped from the chopper.

Free-falling through the air, James gritted his teeth, knowing what awaited him in the next few seconds. Rescue lines weren't bungee cords, and even if the synthetic rope didn't snap and send him plummeting to the ground, he was in for one hell of a whiplash when he reached the end. He heard the helicopter's blades chopping overhead as McCarter tried to estimate the distance.

Then suddenly James felt as if he'd been laid out on the torture rack in some medieval dungeon. The harness bit into his shoulders and crotch, and threatened to rip his limbs from their sockets. His vision blurred, then cleared as most of the pain disappeared. He twirled like a top on the end of the rescue line as the twists worked themselves out. When he finally stopped, he found himself at a forty-five degree angle, racing along next to the cab of the truck like a worm on a trolling line.

The Phoenix Force warrior's eyes jerked toward the compound. They were less than two hundred yards away. He turned back to the open window of the cab and saw Manning watching him from behind the wheel.

The big Canadian turned back to the windshield.

James reached forward and caught the doorframe through the open window. He pulled himself forward, trying to reach the man behind the wheel.

"Wait," the Canadian shouted through the wind.

James pulled himself halfway through the window and grabbed his teammate under the arms. "I'm going nuts. I'd have sworn you said 'wait.'"

Manning nodded as the truck sped on toward the locked gate. "I did. We've got to make sure this thing hits its mark. We can't take any chances."

"Yeah, right," James said as he struggled for a more secure grip. "Like, there's no risk involved in this."

"Get ready," Manning said as the gate raced up to meet them. James saw him reach forward and grab the wrench attached to the end of the wire. "Ready... set...*now!*" He jerked the wire.

James heard the grind of steel against steel as the trailer separated from the tractor. Manning whipped the steering wheel hard to the right as the truck hit the gate, then reached over to loop his arms around James's neck.

Sparks flew like a fireworks display as the electrical circuit running through the chain lengths blew. Gunfire erupted from the towers, pounding into the cab around the two men as James jerked his fellow warrior through the window.

The big Canadian felt like he weighed a thousand pounds during the split second they dangled at the end of the rescue line. Then the weight doubled as McCarter suddenly shot the chopper straight up.

James felt Manning's fingers dig into the tendons in his neck. The former Navy SEAL struggled to hold on as they rose. He glanced down in time to see the trailer hit the farther of the two doors and explode. A fraction of a second later, the tractor met the door directly beneath them and flames, dirt and concrete shot up through the air.

The black Nissan Maxima raced through the gate and skidded to a halt between the doors. Encizo leaped from behind the wheel, Katz from the passenger's seat. Both men took cover behind the car.

The first coughing terrorist stumbled through the door of the compound as McCarter flew over the fence away from the guard towers. Katz and Encizo cut the man down a foot from the building.

As soon as they were out of rifle range, McCarter dropped the chopper until James felt his boots strike the ground. The black Phoenix Force warrior slid out of the harness as the helicopter landed twenty yards away.

More terrorists fled the burning building, falling victims to the autofire from behind the Maxima.

Manning beat James to the chopper. The big Canadian reached behind the seat, jerked out one of the Valmets and sprinted away to join Katz and Encizo.

James jumped on board, grabbing the antitank rifle as McCarter lifted off again, flying high over the compound, then dropping toward the nearest guard tower. The ex-Navy SEAL grasped the pistol grip of the big assault weapon with one hand, working the rack-and-pinion cocking handle with the other. He leaned into the shoulder pad, closed one eye and stared down the sights toward the tower.

A moment later, a 20 x 138B Long Solothurn round left the barrel. The huge bullet hit a flammable substance within the structure and the guard tower went up in flames.

McCarter turned the chopper toward the other tower. As James recocked the weapon, he saw Manning race around the corner of the concrete building. The Canadian took up position at the rear of the fortress. Seconds later, the back door opened and three terrorists raced out holding handkerchiefs over their faces.

Manning cut loose with a steady stream of auto fire, catching the trio chest-high and punching them to the ground.

James sighted on the other guard tower and pulled the trigger. The Lahti exploded again, this time the round striking one of the posts and cutting it crisply in two like some giant power saw.

Screaming voices could be heard above the sound caused by the crashing tower. James drew a bead on the wreckage as it hit the ground and sent another 20 mm round from the Lahti. That one struck home, sending scraps of wood flying through the air.

The gunfire suddenly halted. James looked down to see Katz and Encizo enter the building on one side, Manning on the other. McCarter dropped the helicopter low enough over the guard tower to ascertain that there were no survivors, then landed fifty feet from the building. The Briton jumped out and hurried toward the nearest terrorist. The body lay on its face. He slid a boot under its ribs and rolled it to its side.

The partially blown-away face of a man in his early twenties stared up at him.

James hurried to the three men he'd seen Manning shoot earlier. Two were blond-haired, the third had been short and thin.

The anxiety rose in the Phoenix Force warrior's chest as he turned toward the crumbled guard shacks. There was no point looking there. Dag Vaino would hardly have assigned himself to such duty.

Manning came jogging out of the building, his nose buried in his sleeve. He stopped to take a deep breath, then started toward James. The big Canadian shook his head.

Together, James and Manning rounded the building in time to see Encizo and Katz exit. Both men had wet rags over their faces. They dropped them to the ground as McCarter hurried to join them.

James watched Katz glance back toward the door. The Israeli's weathered face showed pain—not physical pain so much as the pain that comes from pouring your heart, soul and very being into a mission only to accomplish it, then realize it missed the mark.

Slowly Katz turned to face his men. "There's probably forty dead men inside there," he said softly. "But not one of them is Dag Vaino."

Lyons, Schwarz and Blancanales flattened against the walls as gunfire ricocheted around the stairwell. Chips of concrete and dust flew through the air as the automatic 9 mm rounds struck the blocks, then flew through the tiny area like a swarm of angry bees.

Blancanales and Schwarz fired at the landing below while Lyons turned the Python upward, snapping a double-tap of .357s through the rail at the fleeting glimpse of face behind the Uzi. He saw the man fall forward, then the Uzi tumbled down to his feet.

The big ex-cop scooped it off the concrete and ejected the magazine. One lone round remained. He dropped the weapon and drew the suppressed Colt .45 automatic with his left hand as he started up the stairs. His teammates followed, walking backward as they continued firing toward the landing below.

Lyons reached the fifth floor as a scream echoed up to meet his ears. The Berettas quieted and he heard the clink as another subgun hit the floor below.

He opened the door and stepped back.

Automatic fire sailed through the door and pounded the walls. Another ricocheting round blew back to strike him in the thigh. He looked down to see blood seeping through a tear in his pant leg, but the bullet had lost most of its velocity. The wound wasn't deep.

Lyons dropped to one knee as soon as the burst ended and risked a quick glance around the door frame.

The bodies of half a dozen men—the Secret Service agents assigned to the South Haakovians—littered the floor. Three Oriental with Uzis stood shoulder-to-shoulder at the other end of the hall in front of a window.

One of the men spotted him, and a quick burst drove the ex-cop back against the wall. Below, Lyons heard the stairwell door open and shut. Then Blancanales hurried up the steps to his side. "Gadgets is going outside to the ledge."

"Go with him."

"What about—"

"Do it. One man can do as much here as two."

Blancanales turned and hurried back down the steps.

Lyons curled his arm around the corner and double-actioned the Python blindly down the hall. Return fire sailed through the door as he opened the cylinder, dumped the empty brass and dropped a speedloader over the holes. He emptied another six rounds of 125-grain jacketed hollowpoints into the hallway to keep the gunmen busy, holding the .45 in his left hand, at the ready in case another attack came from below.

The Able Team leader reloaded the Python once more as he waited for the noise he expected to hear behind the Chinese gunmen. It came, finally—the sound of a 9 mm slug streaking through glass from the other end of the hall.

Lyons rose to his feet and stepped into the doorway. One of the Chinese lay sprawled on the floor. The other two were in the process of swinging their Uzis toward the window behind them.

Through the glass, Lyons saw Gadgets Schwarz edging along the thin ledge that circled the fifth floor. The ex-cop raised his .357, squeezing the trigger twice and sending two hollowpoints into the spine of the short-haired Oriental who had been on the elevator with Chou. As the man dropped, he saw Schwarz and the remaining gunman fire at each other simultaneously.

Schwarz's 9 mm round took the man in the side of the face. He twirled wildly across the hall, then his shoulder struck the wall and the body slid to the carpet. But at the same time, the burst from the Uzi had found its mark. Gadgets flew back from the window, falling out of sight.

Lyons rushed down the hall toward the splintered glass, fearing the worst. The same ballistic nylon that had saved him on the stairs would have protected him from the 9 mm round.

But the vest hadn't yet been invented that guarded against falls from fifth-story windows.

The Able Team leader ground to a halt at the window, nausea rising from his stomach to his throat as he gripped the ledge and looked down, dreading the sight of Schwarz's crumpled body that he knew he'd see below.

Then his lips curled in a grin as he saw Schwarz dangling against the wall of the Helmsley Palace, two stories down.

The fire hose tied around Gadgets's waist ran up into the hall window of the fourth floor, connecting Able Team's electronics expert to the hotel like some giant umbilical cord.

Schwarz saw Lyons looking down, shook his head and waved the ex-cop away. He began climbing the hose hand over hand as Lyons turned back to the hall.

The Able Team leader stopped over the body of an Oriental wearing a black sport coat and charcoal slacks. He holstered the .45 and Python, then pried the Uzi from the man's dead fingers, ejected the mag and replaced it with a fresh load from the gunman's waistband.

Somewhere, nearby, was Benny Chou. But where?

Lyons walked softly down the hall to room 505. He reached out, twisted the knob and found it locked.

That was okay. Carl Lyons had the key.

As he had done countless times as an LAPD detective, Lyons raised his right foot into the air and kicked it into the door just below the knob. The lock snapped, and the door flew back to reveal an empty room.

Moving to room 507 next door, Lyons kicked again. He found the bodies of two more Secret Service men inside, but no South Haakovian diplomats.

He stopped in front of the door to room 509 as a muffled whimper drifted into the hall. He heard a slap, then another sob. Raising the Uzi to eye-level, he kicked in the door. The sights of Lyons's subgun fell on the bound and gagged body of one of the South Haakovians.

Benny Chou stood directly behind the man, his back pressed against the picture window looking down onto Madison Avenue. Chou had wrapped a forearm around the diplomat's throat. He held the trembling man close to his body, using it as a shield as he dug the muzzle of a Chinese Type 67 7.62 mm automatic deeper into the back of the Haakovian's neck.

The eyes above the taped mouth grimaced in pain.

"Come in, American," Chou said pleasantly. "I was just about to begin." He nodded toward the beds.

Six more of the S.H. delegates lay sprawled across the two mattresses, their hands, feet and mouths bound with white adhesive tape.

Lyons lowered the Uzi to his side. "You'll never make it out of here alive."

Chou smiled. "I am prepared to face death. Are you?"

Lyons didn't bother to answer. A sudden flicker of movement caught his eye through the window. He resisted the impulse to look directly at it. He knew who it was, *what* it was.

And he knew it represented the South Haakovians' only chance.

In the corner of his eye Lyons watched Blancanales creep along the narrow ledge. The Able Team warrior's Beretta was stuffed into his belt, his palms pressed against the window for balance. Lyons knew what he was trying to do.

Pol had to get to an angle where he could shoot Chou without killing the South Haakovian as well.

And Lyons's peripheral vision took in another discomforting fact as he forced his eyes to remain on Chou. Blancanales was "working without a net."

Unlike Schwarz, there was no fire hose wrapped around his waist.

The hit man pointed his pistol toward the bed and said, "You pick, American. Who should die first?"

Lyons held up a hand, stalling. "How about me?"

Chou laughed. "No. I think you should be privileged to watch the others first." His eyes narrowed into slits. "But do not worry. Your time will come."

On the ledge outside the window, Blancanales stopped. Lyons saw his right hand move slowly away from the glass toward his belt.

Chou aimed at the tangled mass of bodies on the bed again. His fingers tightened around the grips of the Type 67.

"Wait!" Lyons said, his mind racing for another delaying tactic. "There might just be a way to get what you want done and get you out of here in one piece."

A flicker of indecision came over the killer's face.

Lyons saw Blancanales pull the Beretta slowly from his belt, and went on. "I can help you," he told Chou. "If you leave with me, it'll look like I've got you in custody."

"It will never work."

"Oh, there's a few details to iron out," Lyons said. "But that can be done."

Blancanales pressed the barrel of the Beretta against the glass.

"You would betray your country to save your own life?" Chou asked incredulously.

"Hey, in a heartbeat if that's what it comes down to."

Chou spit on the carpet. "That is what I hate about you Americans. Your absolute absence of loyalty is revolting."

"Sure. But it will work to your advantage."

Lyons saw Blancanales take a deep breath. A split second later, he heard the blast of the pistol against the glass. The window shattered, and Bin "Benny" Chou crashed to the floor.

The big ex-cop walked forward, knelt and took the pistol out of Chou's hand. "Just for the record," he said. "I was lying."

SOMEWHERE in the blackened waters of the Inge River, between the northern shore and where Bolan stood to the south, a fish jumped. The man known as the Executioner watched the ripples expand, then disappear as they reached the bank.

Bolan turned and walked back through the tall grass toward the LAV-25 hidden in the trees. For now, another lull had come in the war between North and South Haakovia. But he knew what that lull represented.

Franzen Stensvik was regrouping once more, confident that he would eventually defeat the democratic government to his south.

Bolan entered the trees and walked along the path toward the LAV. Tents had been set up to the side, and the Executioner watched the men from the armored personnel carrier as they sat whispering next to the canvas or eating their cold MREs in the bitter chill of the early-morning hours.

No, the war wasn't over yet. Not by a long shot. As he stopped outside the LAV and pressed his back against the cold hard steel, the Executioner wondered if it ever would be.

The problem had not changed since the beginning of the turmoil between the two countries. If the South defeated Stensvik, what would prevent the man from launching a nuclear attack with the weapons he had inherited from the Soviets? Add to that the fact that they now knew he had secret caches of biological agents scattered across the globe, and you found yourself in a catch-22 that seemed to have no answer.

Did you let the North win and take over through conventional warfare, or defeat them and let a madman destroy everything with his nukes and poison?

Neither was a viable solution.

Two young Marines walked past, their faces reflecting the eagerness to get on with the war, if war was what would be. They nodded, knowing better than to salute an officer in the field, and the Executioner nodded back. He knew how they felt. The waiting was always the hard part.

The flickering image of a raven-haired woman crossed the Executioner's mind. He had built emotional defenses around himself like a fortress over the years. In his quest against evil, he had known he couldn't afford the distraction from duty that love brought with it. But even the best defenses had holes. And Janyte Varkaus was brushing up against his protective shield. He'd have to keep his distance emotionally.

He glanced at the glowing hands of his watch. Right now, she would be asleep. He would call anyway. He needed to make sure the castle guard was in place around her temporary quarters, and answer any questions regarding her security during his absence at the front lines.

Bolan climbed onto the LAV, dropped down through the hatch and lifted the cellular phone from the console next to the command chair. He climbed out of the vehicle again and walked back toward the river, stopping to drop down onto a large boulder a few feet from the water.

Moonlight fell across the Inge, bathing it in a warm glow that seemed to contradict the bloodshed that had taken place along its banks. Tiny waves broke against the shore. Bolan tapped Janyte's private number into the instrument, pressed the receiver against his ear and let it ring.

There was no answer.

The uneasiness in his chest started slowly, then grew. Okay, she wasn't answering the phone. That didn't mean anything was wrong. The woman had been through hell and was exhausted. She could be so sound asleep that the phone didn't wake her. Or she could be in the bathroom.

But the warrior doubted it. Something was wrong.

He tapped the number for the castle-guard station into the phone. It was answered on the first ring.

"Captain Volandermar," a husky voice said.

"This is Pollock. Where is the president?"

Volandermar didn't hesitate. "In her quarters, Colonel. Have you tried her private number?"

"I have. No answer."

"That's very strange. General Markus and a Finnish military adviser visited her only a few minutes ago. They borrowed four of my men to help carry the records, and said she was fine when he left."

Bolan's uneasiness crystallized into reality in a heartbeat. "What records?"

This time, Volandermar did hesitate. "I don't know, sir. I didn't ask. But there must have been a lot of them. One of the men said the trunk they carried from the president's chambers almost broke his back."

There was no need for the warrior to ask what the man with Markus had looked like. He didn't have to. The man was a master of disguise, and however he had dressed, whether he'd had a mustache, a beard, a clean-shaved face or eyeglasses, the Executioner knew who it had been with General Markus.

Dag Vaino.

Janyte Varkaus, the president of South Haakovia, was in the hands of the enemy.

The forces of South Haakovia had been successful thus far in its battles against the North. But the Executioner knew that the real war had just begun.

* * * * *

Don't miss the heart-stopping conclusion of The Freedom Trilogy: Battle Force, *coming in August.*

Take
4 explosive books
plus a
mystery bonus
FREE